# JELLY BABY

# JELLY BABY

## Jean Ure

HarperCollins *Children's Books*

First published in Great Britain by HarperCollins *Children's Books* in 2014
HarperCollins *Children's Books* is a division of HarperCollins*Publishers* Ltd,
77-85 Fulham Palace Road, Hammersmith, London, W6 8JB.

Visit us on the web at
www.harpercollins.co.uk

1

978-0-00-751869-2

Printed and bound in England by
Clays Ltd, St Ives plc

MIX
Paper from
responsible sources
FSC www.fsc.org FSC C007454

FSC™ is a non-profit international organisation established to promote
the responsible management of the world's forests. Products carrying the
FSC label are independently certified to assure consumers that they come
from forests that are managed to meet the social, economic and
ecological needs of present and future generations,
and other controlled sources.

Find out more about HarperCollins and the environment at
**www.harpercollins.co.uk/green**

*For Zoe Cross, because she apologised*

# CHAPTER ONE

"Right, girls!" Cass clapped her hands. "Big clean-up! Let's get started."

Em and I pulled faces. We weren't used to doing housework! Cass is our auntie, and very easy-going. All the time she'd lived with us we'd just bumbled along in one big happy muddle. Now, suddenly, we had an emergency – today was the day when Dad's new girlfriend was coming to dinner!

"You can stop all the huffing and puffing," said Cass. "I want this place spotless! Who wants to dust, who wants to hoover?"

"Bags hoover," I said. I like hoovering, specially when there's lots of empty carpet. I'm not so keen on having to move things. Chairs and stuff. Mostly I don't bother; I just go round them.

Cass pushed the vacuum cleaner towards me. "There you go. OK, Em, seems like you're doing the dusting."

Em gave me a venomous glare. She's my big sister, so she probably thought she was the one that should have been allowed to choose.

"Here you are." Cass tossed the sleeve of an old sweater at her. Sleeves of old sweaters were what we tended to use for dusting. Also socks with holes, and worn-out shirts. "Why waste money on proper dusters?" is what Cass used to say. She's totally into recycling.

Em flicked half-heartedly with her old sweater sleeve.

"I'll need a bit more energy than that!" said Cass. "And you, Bitsy." She nodded sternly at me. "No missing out on corners."

I said, "You can't get *into* corners. Anyway, we did all this when Dad had his party." Dad had invited everybody that worked in his department at college, and we had dusted and vacuumed all over the place. Why do it again so soon after?

"For your information," said Cass, "your dad's party was way back last month."

"Was it?" I said. "Blimey!"

"I know," said Cass, "it's appalling. Most people do it once a week."

"No, I meant blimey, it doesn't seem that long ago."

"Well, it is, so just get on with it."

"What are you going to do?" said Em.

Cass cast her eye about the room. "I am going to

clear up all this *stuff*." She waved a hand at the dining table, which is hardly ever used as a dining table since we usually eat in the kitchen. As a result it is permanently covered in what Cass calls *clutter*. A big pile of clothes, waiting to be ironed. Someone's school bag. Someone's homework. Someone's trainers. Books. Newspapers. Bananas. *Bananas?*

"Where does it all come from?" said Cass. "More importantly," she added, "where is it all supposed to *go?*"

She began picking things up and throwing them into a bin bag. Em and I let out immediate wails.

"Those are my trainers!"

"That's my homework!"

"Just for now, just for now." Trainers and homework were tossed into the bag. "You can take them out later."

On top of the ironing was a big fat fur ball, happily snoozing. It was Bella, our cat. She does a lot of snoozing.

"You can't move her," said Em. "Not when she's settled."

"Pardon *me*," said Cass. "Some of us have work to do." With that she plucked poor Bella off the ironing and deposited her, rather rudely I thought, on the sofa. Bella sat up, looking shocked.

"That's cruel," I said. How would Cass like it if someone plucked her out of her nice cosy bed and plonked her down somewhere else?

"Can't help it." Cass swept up the ironing and flung it in the bag. "Got to make the place look decent. We don't want Caroline thinking we live in a tip."

Caroline was the name of Dad's girlfriend. Caroline Scott-Mason. Very grand!

"Cass is right," said Em. "We have to make a *bit* of an effort. It's only fair."

She meant fair to Dad. It was ages since he'd had a girlfriend. Unless you counted Polly. Polly was one of the lecturers in his department at college, and for a while we'd had what Cass called High Hopes. And then Caroline had come along. It wasn't that we didn't like Caroline, what little we'd seen of her. We liked her a lot! It's just that we'd known Polly for ever. She'd been there for us all those years ago when Mum had died, before Cass had moved in to look after us. Cass said Dad had probably known her too long and as a result he took her for granted.

"It's just one of those things. Polly's like an old comfortable slipper; Caroline is new and exciting. You can't blame your dad. He was devastated when he lost your mum. It's not surprising if he's behaving like a lovesick teenager."

*Was* he? Perhaps he was. I giggled.

"Come on," said Cass. "Give him a break!"

Cass is Dad's sister and fiercely loyal. She said it was about time Dad found some happiness in his life. "Goodness knows, he's waited long enough."

"I agree," said Em. She gave me one of her looks.

What I call her *big sister look*. Very quickly I said that I agreed too. Cos I did! I was just as anxious as anyone else for Dad to be happy. It was the only reason we were all working so hard to make the evening a success. For Dad's sake. Nothing else would have had me whizzing around with the vacuum cleaner at five o'clock on a Saturday afternoon without grumbling about it!

I personally consider housework to be a total waste of time, not to mention energy. To my way of thinking, a bit of mess and clutter makes a place more comfortable, but I had this feeling Caroline might be the sort of person that thinks tidiness is important.

I jumped up and flapped my hand at a cobweb hanging off the lampshade. Caroline wouldn't approve of cobwebs! The two times we'd met her we'd been, like, gobsmacked. How did Dad get a girlfriend like that? Smart and sassy, dressed like she'd just stepped off the catwalk. Dad is the least smart person in the world.

Left to himself he would shamble around in the same old baggy joggers and faded sweatshirt until they fell to pieces. And even then he probably wouldn't notice! He is really not into fashion at all.

We were quite surprised when he poked his head round the sitting-room door to announce that he was going off to fetch Caroline and we saw that he was all dressed up.

"Dad!" I left off vacuuming and skipped sideways to get a better look. "You're wearing proper trousers!"

Dad shuffled, obviously embarrassed.

"Don't tease him," said Cass. "He wants to look nice. He *does* look nice!"

"I didn't even know you *had* that jacket," said Em.

"Been in the cupboard for years," muttered Dad. "Thought I'd better give it a go before the moths got at it."

"Quite right too," said Cass.

"So, um… how's it going?" said Dad.

"All under control. Don't worry! As soon as we've

finished in here we're going to start preparing dinner. Right, you two?"

"Right." We nodded. A faint look of alarm had spread across Dad's face.

"You mean, you haven't actually cooked anything yet?"

"It's only just gone five," said Cass. "We're aiming for seven o'clock. Yes? Yes! So off you go." She gave Dad a little push. "We'll see you back here at six thirty. Just stop panicking! We've got it all planned."

"If you say so," said Dad. He still didn't sound too certain.

"I do say so! Will you please just *go?*"

"You're making us nervous," said Em.

"Sorry," said Dad. "Sorry, sorry! I'll get out of your hair."

He disappeared and we heard the front door open and close. I giggled. "I think Dad's the one that's nervous!"

Cass said, "He is, bless him. Like a boy on his first date! Let's go and make a start on the food."

We'd already decided what we were going to

do – steak and kidney pie followed by lemon possets. *Mock* steak and kidney, that is. Thanks to Cass, we had all become vegetarian ages ago. So instead of steak we used Quorn pieces, and instead of kidney we had brown mushrooms. Chestnut mushrooms, I think they are called. With mashed potatoes and gravy, and pastry on top, it is very yummy! Nobody would ever guess it didn't have meat in it.

"Bags I do the potatoes!" I said.

"That's not fair," said Em. "You already got to do the vacuuming. It's my turn to choose… *I'll* do the potatoes, you do the onions."

Ugh! Yuck. Onions make your eyes water.

"You do the garlic, then," I said.

"No way! Whoever does the onions does the garlic as well. You can always roll out the pastry," she added, "if you like."

"Oh, all right," I said.

She was being quite generous, cos we both enjoy rolling out pastry.

"Know what?" said Cass, setting down the frying pan. "I'm starting to have second thoughts... I'm wondering if we should have real meat, as it's a guest."

We both stared at her, shocked. I could hardly believe what I was hearing!

"You mean cook dead *animal*?" said Em.

Cass did look a bit ashamed. "Only because it's so important to your dad," she pleaded.

"We don't do meat when Gran comes," I said.

"Gran's not his girlfriend."

"Ladyfriend, *actually*," said Em.

"Whatever." Cass waved a hand. "It seems only polite."

"But it's a *principle*," said Em. "You don't break a principle just to be polite!"

"In any case," I said, "we haven't got any meat." I giggled. "Unless we give her cat food!"

"I could always pop up the road and buy a tin of stewing steak."

"I'm not going to eat stewing steak," said Em.

"Nor 'm I," I said, though I really only said it to support Em. I would never have admitted it to her, but every now and again, at school, I was almost tempted to let my friend Lottie feed me a bite of something meaty as a sort of dare, just to see what it tasted like. I mean, I wasn't scared of it or anything. But it's really important to Em. She is into animals in a big way.

"Maybe I should do *two* pies," said Cass. "One for Caroline and one for the rest of us."

"If you do that," said Em, chucking her potato peeler across the draining board, "I refuse to help."

Cass sighed. It's rare for Em to throw a tantrum. She is not at all a rebellious sort of person. It's just that she has these really strong feelings.

"Honestly," I said, "nobody's ever going to know it's not real meat. We could pretend it's chicken… chicken and mushroom!"

"I don't think we can actually lie about it," said Cass.

"On the other hand we don't actually have to *say* that it's not meat." She suddenly cheered up. "We'll make the gravy nice and strong! That'll help."

"Yes, and we've got my lemon possets for after," I said. "Everybody loves those!"

I'd made the possets myself. It is my special pudding that I do. Cream, sugar and lemon juice, all whisked up and poured into little separate dishes. I am quite proud of my lemon possets! They are what Cass calls *gourmet*, meaning, like, very refined. Not just some old rubbish out of a tin.

I reckoned the whole meal was going to be *gourmet*, what with the dining table being cleared of clutter and laid out all posh and proper with place mats and sparkly glasses, and the cutlery checked to make sure there weren't any bits of old food mouldering on it, which is what sometimes happens when me and Cass do the washing-up.

Em says we are slapdash. When she washes up she is very slow and careful. I get quite impatient! I keep trying to snatch things from her so I can get on with wiping them. This leads to breakages. We break a lot of things in our house. It is one of the reasons we tend not to have any matching plates or glasses.

Dad isn't so much slapdash as clumsy. He managed to shatter a glass the other day just breathing on it. Well, that is what he claimed.

"I didn't go anywhere near it!" he had said.

Dad is pretty useless, really, at everything except teaching people history. He can't even change a plug without nearly electrocuting himself. But he is a very *intelligent* person. Perhaps that was why Caroline had fallen for him. She must have realised from the word go that he was not very clever at the ordinary, everyday things of life, since the way they met was when Dad reversed into her *twice* in the underground car park! He is not the world's best driver. According to Cass, he could even be the world's worst.

Poor Dad! He really did need looking after. It was

why we were all working so hard to make the evening a success. Just because Dad was hopeless it didn't mean the rest of us were.

Now that we'd finally settled on what to cook, Cass started to fret about not having a proper wine glass for Caroline to drink out of.

"I thought *that* was a wine glass," I said. I pointed to one that I'd spent ages polishing with a bit of old sheet that we used for wiping up. "It looks like one."

"Actually," said Cass, "it's a sherry glass."

"Sherry is wine," said Em.

"Not *table* wine. Oh, God, why didn't I think of it before? I could have picked some up on my way home!"

"We'd only go and break them," I said.

Cass ran her fingers through her hair, bunching it up on top of her head.

"This is serious! Caroline's not the sort of person to drink wine out of an ordinary tumbler."

"So why can't she drink it out of the sherry glass? It's ever such a nice shape!"

Cass said, "But it's not a wine glass! It wouldn't hold more than a thimbleful."

I honestly couldn't see what all the fuss was about. A glass is a glass, seems to me.

"They're very *pretty* tumblers," I said. Gran had given them to us last Christmas. "And look, there's loads of them!"

"They're still tumblers." Cass took her fingers out of her hair, leaving it sticking up like a haystack. "Sophisticated people don't drink wine out of tumblers."

I said, "Oh." Caroline was definitely a sophisticated person.

"I don't want her thinking your dad's some kind of oik. And omigod! What about plates? Do we have five plates?"

Em rushed to have a look. "There are five with roses," she said, "but two of them are chipped."

Cass let out a little scream. Me and Em exchanged glances. Em shook her head. Cass is usually such a calm sort of person. Very laid-back, like Dad. I was really surprised it bothered her so much. I mean... once the food was on them, what did it matter?

"You can always give the bad ones to me and Em," I said, trying to be helpful. "We won't mind."

"She'll still notice," moaned Cass. "I'm sorry, girls, I know you think I'm making a fuss over nothing, but I feel so bad for your dad. I feel like I'm letting him down."

Me and Em stayed silent.

"Thing is," said Em at last, "it's Dad she's supposed to be in love with. Not plates and glasses and stuff."

"This is it," I said. "If I was in love with somebody I wouldn't care what they ate off. They could eat off newspaper. They could eat off the floor! Wouldn't make any difference to me."

"I would think it's a bit pathetic," said Em. "Getting all worked up about that sort of thing."

Sadly, Cass said, "That just shows what sort of upbringing you've had. I've been a poor substitute for a mother!"

We both immediately rushed to reassure her.

"You've taught us to care about the things that really matter," said Em. "Like not eating animals, and—"

She stopped and rather frantically rolled an eye in my direction. I dived in to her rescue.

"And not wasting your life doing boring things like housework!"

Cass smiled and shook her head. "Oh dear," she said. "What a legacy! Never mind." She picked up the mock steak and kidney and popped it into the oven. "It's a bit too late to do anything about it now. I suggest you two go and get changed. Your dad will be bringing Caroline back at any moment."

"Why have we got to change?" said Em. "What's wrong with the way we are?"

"Well, for one thing," said Cass, "you're covered in flour. Just go and find something clean! You want your dad to be proud of you, don't you?"

"Got to be smart for Caroline," I cried, as we hurtled upstairs.

I knew exactly what I was going to wear. I had this favourite skirt, bright red with pleats, like a mini kilt. Really short. I mean, like, *really* short. My friend Lottie had one too; we'd bought them at the same time. Lottie's mum had taken one look and gone, "Oh, to be eleven years old again! What I wouldn't give to be able to wear something like that."

Lottie, being kind, said, "Mum, you still could!" but her mum said no.

"They're for little young people, not middle-aged mums."

As I stood in front of my wardrobe mirror, admiring myself, there came an anguished wail from Em's room.

"Hey, Bitsy!"

"What?"

I went on to the landing. Em appeared, trailing garments.

"Oh," she said, "you've got your skirt on. I adore that skirt!"

"You ought to get one," I said.

Not that we could have worn them at the same time. Well, if they were different colours I suppose we could. Me and Lottie did. But Em rather sadly said, "It would just look stupid on me. I'm the wrong sort of shape."

It's true that Em is a bit tall and gangly, and somewhat on the skinny side, whereas I am short and – not *dumpy*. But kind of… well! Roundish.

"So what are you going to wear?" I said.

"I don't know!" Em held up the various garments she'd pulled out of her wardrobe. "What do you think? Would these do?"

She waved a pair of jeans at me. I inspected them critically. I am not an expert in fashion. Fashion is not really something that plays much of a part in our lives. As far as Dad and Cass are concerned, it doesn't even exist. But I do have a bit more of a clue than Em. Being long and skinny, Em is very sensitive about her appearance. She doesn't have much confidence. Even though she is two years older than I am she is always turning to me for advice.

Anxiously, she said, "So what do you think?"

"Jeans'll be OK," I said. "So long as you have a nice top."

"This?"

She held up a big chunky sweater that Gran had knitted for her. Em likes big chunky sweaters – she reckons they'll hide the fact that she doesn't have any bosom. I told her yes, OK, cos I mean there is absolutely no sense trying to turn people into something they are not. And in any case, Cass always says it's important to feel comfortable in your clothes. Dress Em up like a model and she would just die of embarrassment.

"Are you sure?" she said. "I wouldn't want Dad being ashamed of me! I—"

"Yes, yes, yes!" I hustled her back into her room. "Just get dressed… quickly. That was Dad's car. They're here!"

# CHAPTER TWO

We hurtled downstairs just in time to greet Dad and Caroline as they came through the door.

"Everything's on!" I cried. I wanted to set Dad's mind at rest – I knew how anxious he was. "It's being cooked right now."

"Whatever it is," said Caroline, "it smells delicious."

"It's a pie," I said. "Steak and kidney!"

"Ooh, yum! Exactly what one needs on a cold night."

I beamed. "That's what we thought."

Dad said, "Jolly good! Steak and kidney, eh?"

"Well, you know... *m*—"

I was about to say *mock* steak and kidney, but I suddenly remembered that we were hoping Caroline would think it was chicken.

"Actually, I forgot," I said. "It was *going* to be steak and kidney, but then at the last minute we changed it to chicken and mushroom."

"Still sounds delicious," said Caroline.

"It will be," I promised. "Cass is a really good cook!"

"Yes. Well." Dad sounded as if he wasn't quite sure what to make of everything. "Bitsy, could you take Caroline's coat and hang it somewhere?"

I said, "Where?"

"In the – um – closet?" said Dad.

What closet? I didn't know what a closet was! I didn't think we had one. We usually draped coats and stuff over the banisters, but maybe Caroline wouldn't like that.

"I'll take it upstairs," I said.

I cantered back up. When I came down I found Em hovering.

"We weren't supposed to lie," she hissed.

"'bout what?"

"The pie! Cass said… she didn't think we ought to lie about it."

"I didn't lie!"

"Yes, you did, you said it was chicken and mushroom."

"That's all right. Soon as we've finished I'll tell her the truth." I giggled. "She won't half be surprised!"

"She might be cross," said Em. "I would be, like, if someone gave me meat and pretended it was something else."

"That's cos you've got principles," I said. "People don't have principles about eating vegetables."

"All the same," said Em.

Oh dear! Em is such a worrier.

We went into the sitting room to find Caroline holding out my sherry glass I'd so lovingly polished so that Dad could pour sherry into it. Hah! I knew it would come in useful.

"Do you think Cass would like any help in the kitchen?" she said.

Dad very quickly said, "No, no! And if she does the girls are here to give her a hand."

He probably didn't want Caroline seeing the mess the kitchen was in. We always make a mess when we cook. I reckon all the best chefs do.

"I'll go," said Em. She pulled a face at me as she left the room. She was going to tell Cass that I'd pretended we were having real chicken in the pie. I just knew she was. Well, so what? I bet when people eat in restaurants they're given all sorts of stuff they don't get told about.

I went over to the sofa to sit with Caroline.

"My," she said, "that is a real miniskirt, isn't it. What you might call a *mini* miniskirt!"

Dad looked at me like it was the first time he'd ever seen it.

"It is a bit on the short side," he said. "Did Cass buy it for you?"

I said, "No, I bought it for myself. Lottie's got one as well. I've had it for *ages*."

"You presumably don't go out in it?" said Caroline.

"I should hope not!" said Dad.

"I…" I hesitated, not quite sure what to say. Was there something wrong with going out in it? I was saved by Cass coming through from the kitchen.

She said, "Oh really, Donald! Don't be such a prude. She always wears leggings with it, or thick tights. Absolutely nothing to get fussed about! Hello, Caroline. Good to see you again. Dinner won't be long; just finishing it off."

Dad, sounding puzzled, said, "If she's had it all this time, why haven't I seen it before?"

"Because you go round with your eyes closed," said Cass. "I'm afraid, Caroline, this brother of mine is so wrapped up in the eighteenth century he really has no idea what's going on in the real world."

Caroline laughed. She said, "Tell me about it! Anyone who can reverse into somebody twice in just two minutes…"

I liked that she could laugh about Dad reversing into her. Not everybody would. She was obviously a very tolerant, good-natured sort of person. Not someone who would lose patience with Dad when he couldn't find his front-door key or forgot to put petrol in the car, *both* of which had happened in the past week. I decided that Caroline was exactly what he needed!

I was glad, though, that Cass had spoken up in defence of my skirt. Just for a minute I had started to feel a bit self-conscious, thinking that maybe it was indecent or something. I knew it couldn't be, or Lottie's mum would never have let Lottie buy one. As mums go, she is quite strict. But I didn't want Caroline to think badly of me. At school recently we'd been discussing role models and I'd decided that that's what Caroline was – my role model. She was so smart, and so cool, and so... sophisticated! I really wanted to make a good impression on her.

Em stuck her head round the door and said, "Shall I start bringing things in?"

"I'll help!" I went racing after her into the kitchen. "I suppose you went and told her?" I hissed.

"Told her what?"

"About me saying it was chicken and mushroom!"

"All I said," said Em, "was are we supposed to be telling her the truth or not? OK? Here! Take the sprouts. And *don't go dropping them.*"

"Oh, this looks very tasty," said Caroline, as we all took our places. The pie sat steaming in its dish, the top all beautifully brown and crusty, with little pastry roses decorating it. Cass had gone to *such* a lot of trouble.

"I hope it meets with your approval," she said,

passing Caroline a plate. "I don't want to mislead you… it's not actually real chicken."

"It's not?" said Dad. He sounded a bit put out. "Bitsy? I thought you said it was!"

Em looked at me, rather hard.

"Just for once," said Dad, "it might have been nice." He turned apologetically to Caroline. "I'm afraid I live in a house full of mad veggies," he said.

"You're one too!" cried Em.

"Not through choice," said Dad. "They bully me, you know. I have no say in the matter, I just have to eat what I'm given."

"I'm sure it will still be delicious," said Caroline.

I kept shooting little glances at her as she ate. I *think* she enjoyed it. At any rate, she cleared her plate. She didn't come back for seconds, though. I did! But I am quite a greedy sort of person. You don't get to be as slim as Caroline by gorging yourself.

Triumphantly, as Cass began to clear away the

dishes, I said, "If you hadn't been told it wasn't chicken I bet you wouldn't have known, would you?"

"Well… I think I probably would have done," said Caroline, "but that doesn't mean it wasn't very lovely."

"But how could you tell?" I said. "It *looks* like chicken."

"I suppose it doesn't quite… taste like it."

"Chicken tastes of blood," said Em.

"Oh, for goodness' sake!" Dad threw up his hands. "Do we have to?"

"I'm just saying," said Em. "It's full of stale blood."

"Em!" Cass jerked her head. "Help me take the dishes out."

I jumped up. "I'll go and get the pudding!"

I was *so* proud of my possets. I carried them through triumphantly on a tray.

"Bitsy made these herself," said Cass.

"Ah, the famous possets!" Dad rubbed his hands. "They always go down well."

I said, "Yes, cos it's *real* lemon and *real* sugar and *real* cream."

"What else could it be?" said Em.

"Could be soya cream."

"Oh! I never thought of that. Maybe next time—"

"*No.*" Dad snatched a couple of pots and handed one to Caroline. "Don't go and ruin a good thing."

"I just thought—"

"Not now," said Cass. "Let Caroline enjoy her pudding."

As soon as I started on my posset, Bella appeared. With one bound she was up beside me, nearly pulling the tablecloth off in the process.

"Good gracious," said Caroline. "A *cat* on the table?"

Dad frowned. "Bitsy, put her down."

"Dad!" Em looked at him reproachfully. "You know we don't say that. She'll think we're taking her to the vet to be…"

"Murdered," I said.

"Euthanised," said Dad.

"It means the same thing!" Em was getting quite worked up. "Just don't *say* it."

Em is very protective where Bella is concerned. Well, with all animals, really. She is going to be a vet when she grows up.

Dad shook his head, like, *What can you do?* "Just put her on the floor," he said. "We don't have cats up here while we're eating."

I opened my mouth to object cos, I mean, Bella is used to joining us on the table no matter what Dad said, but Cass, sitting next to me, gave me a warning jab.

"Just do what your dad says."

I set Bella on the ground. She immediately jumped back up again.

Dad said, "Bitsy…"

I said, "Yes, all right! She just wants a bit of posset." I dug out a blob with my finger and gave it to her to lick. She purred appreciatively. "Lemon possets are one of her favourites," I said. "She'd live on them if she could!"

Caroline said, "Really? It surely can't be good for her."

"It's the cream," I said. "Cats love cream."

"But it's so fattening! No wonder she has a bit of a tum."

It was true, I suppose. Bella's tummy does sometimes wobble slightly as she walks.

"She's not *fat*," I said earnestly. "It's mostly fur. Feel!" I held Bella out to her, but Dad intervened.

"I did tell you, Bitsy, to put her on the floor."

"I'll put her on the sofa," I said. "She'll be happy there. When we first had her," I told Caroline, "we called her Belle o' the Ball. Now Dad says she's Bella the Ball! But she does have *very* thick fur." I added this quickly before Em could give me another of her looks. Bella is mainly her cat and she won't let anyone say anything bad about her.

"Well, now," said Cass, "if everyone's eaten enough I'll go and put the coffee on. Bits, do you want to give me a hand?"

"Caroline hasn't finished!" I said. She'd only eaten half her posset.

"No, no, I'm through." Caroline pushed her plate away from her. "It was lovely, but I'm just too full up after all that pie."

"I don't think she liked it," I whispered to Cass as we went through to the kitchen.

"Oh, she's just worried about putting on a few extra kilos," said Cass. "She'd probably have been far happier with a glass of water and a couple of grapes. *Peeled.*"

I gazed at Cass doubtfully, not sure whether she was being serious or just joking.

"Stop looking so woebegone!" Cass gave me a hug. "She's a very figure-conscious lady... I bet she won't take either milk or sugar in her coffee! Go and check with her."

I skipped back into the sitting room to see Caroline lowering herself into one of the armchairs. As she did so, she gave a little squeak.

"Ooh, what's this?"

Gingerly she slid her hand down the side and held something up.

"Oh!" I said. "My dividers! From my geometry set. I wondered where they'd gone."

Dad, rather crossly, said, "For goodness' sake, Bitsy! You really must be more careful. That could have caused a nasty accident."

Embarrassed, I muttered that I was very sorry.

"Not to worry," said Caroline. "No harm done. Tell me, as a matter of interest, why does everyone call you Bitsy when your name is Flora?"

Em said, "Hah!"

"You can tell her," I said, "if you want." She was obviously bursting to.

"OK! It's cos once when she was little," explained Em, "Dad asked Cass if we had any bitter chocolate. He said he really fancied some bitter chocolate. So Cass said we didn't have any cos, like, nobody had ever asked for it before, so *Flora* goes toddling off and comes back all triumphant with two squares of Cadbury's milk saying, 'Look, Dad, bit o' chocolate!'"

"And she's been Bitsy ever since," said Dad fondly.

"Well, it's a sweet story," said Caroline, "but I'm going to call her Flora. I think it's a pity to have such a pretty name and not use it! Like Emily. That's another pretty name." She smiled at us. "Emily and Flora! How about it?"

"You can always try," said Cass.

"I intend to!"

I wondered how I would feel about being called Flora after being Bitsy for so long. Everyone called me Bitsy! Well, not teachers, of course, but everyone in my class. Maybe if I was Flora I would have a bit more dignity, instead of just being a small round person that no one took any notice of.

After Dad had left to take Caroline home, we all sat round discussing how the evening had gone. Had it been a success? Sadly, we came to the conclusion that it hadn't.

"I *know* she didn't like her pudding," I said. "Anyone that really enjoyed it would have gobbled up the whole pot. They wouldn't be able to help it!"

Cass sighed and said she probably hadn't enjoyed her mock pie, either. "It was a big mistake. I should have given her real meat."

"But this is a meat-free zone," said Em.

"But she was our guest!"

"I just don't see how anyone could tell that it *wasn't* real meat," I said. "Not if they hadn't been told."

"Course, you know what really didn't help?" said Em. "Someone going and leaving half their geometry set down the side of the chair. Imagine if she'd got stabbed in an artery!"

"Well, but she *didn't*," I said.

"She could have done."

"Well, but she *didn't*."

"To think we spent all that time tidying up," sighed Cass. "How did we manage to miss it? And then letting that cat jump on the table!"

Em immediately sprang to Bella's defence. "You can't blame Bella! She always jumps on the table."

"You didn't have to go and feed her."

"I didn't feed her!" Em sent me a venomous stare. "*She* did."

"Well, she shouldn't," said Cass. "It's not good for her. You heard what Caroline said... she's getting fat."

"She is not!" Em snatched Bella off the sofa and cradled her lovingly in her arms. "She's just right!"

"I don't care, she still shouldn't be on the table. And we shouldn't *have* to spend hours tidying up. The place should never be allowed to get in that state to begin with. What on earth must she think of us?"

We were all very crestfallen. Normally we'd have left the washing-up till morning, but for once, without even having to be asked, me and Em got started on it straight away, while Cass cleaned up the kitchen. After that, still rather subdued, we went to bed. Em was clutching Bella; I for some reason was clutching my geometry set. I was going to have nightmares now, thinking of Caroline being stabbed in an artery.

In fact I must have fallen asleep the minute my head touched the pillow and gone on sleeping all night, cos the next thing I knew, it was morning and Em was telling me to get up.

"Dad has something he wants to discuss with us... something important. About Caroline!"

# CHAPTER THREE

"I've had a word with Cass," said Dad. "Now I need to have a word with you two."

We both turned wonderingly to Cass in search of clues.

"It's all right," said Cass. "You don't have to look so apprehensive! It's actually something quite exciting. OK,

I'm off to work; Becky's expecting me at the shop. I'll see you all later."

Dad waited until Cass had gone, then very solemnly told us to sit down.

"This is important. I need your full attention."

*Something exciting*, Cass had said. For one mad moment I had this fantasy that we had won the lottery and that Dad was going to ask us how we thought we should spend the money.

"OK! Right. Now! How would you feel," said Dad, "about Caroline moving in?"

We gaped. I could feel my mouth dropping open.

"You mean, like… to live with us?"

"To live with us. Yes!"

"She wants to live *here*?" said Em.

"As part of the family."

"You mean… she's not cross with us?"

"Cross?" Dad seemed puzzled. "Why should she be cross?"

"About Bella jumping on the table?" I said.

"And nearly getting stabbed in an artery," added Em.

"*And* not liking her dinner."

"Oh, now, it wasn't as bad as that," said Dad. "It wasn't that she didn't like it, just that she's not used to vegetarian food. We should have discussed it! I don't think it would have hurt to bend the rules just this one time."

Em opened her mouth to protest, but Dad rushed on. "As for the other things – well! They were just unfortunate. But no harm done, and of course she wasn't cross! She's not the sort of person who gets cross. If she were, she'd have been pretty cross with me reversing into her, don't you think?"

"I guess," said Em.

"At any rate," said Dad, "it hasn't put her off. It's something we've been talking about for a while now. The people she's renting her flat from want it back, so…" Dad giggled. He did! He *giggled*. I'd never seen him so happy and excited. "It seems like the ideal opportunity. What do you reckon?"

Em and I sat there at either end of the sofa, not sure what to say.

Em found her voice. "What does Cass think?"

"She's fine with it," said Dad. "But I'm more anxious to know how you feel."

Earnestly Em said, "We just want you to be happy."

"Yes, but I want *you* to be happy," said Dad. "After all, we're a family."

"Will it mean you're going to get married?" I said.

"That's the plan! If all goes well. And I can't see any reason..." Dad came over to sit between us on the sofa. He put an arm round each of us, pulling us close. "I can't see any reason why it shouldn't. We all seem to get along all right. Don't we?"

We assured him that we did.

"Well, then!" Dad sat back, beaming. "Let's give it a go, shall we, and see what happens?"

On Monday, at school, I told Lottie about Caroline coming to live with us. Lottie was all ears! She knew about Caroline. Me and Lottie always tell each other everything.

"So that's it," I said. "She's moving in."

Lottie's eyes went big as dinner plates. "*Living* with you?"

"Cos the people that own her flat want it back. Well, and cos she and Dad think it's a good idea."

"Does that mean they'll get married?"

"Prob'ly."

Lottie said, "Cool! Then you can be a bridesmaid."

"If all goes well," I said.

Lottie gazed at me, head to one side, her nose sort of scrunched. It's what she does when she's trying to figure things out, like, *Why shouldn't things go well?* She has this really tiny little blob of a nose like a lump of Play-Doh. It makes her look seriously silly!

"D'you want them to?"

"To get married?" I thought about it. *Did* I want them to? I did for Dad's sake. It was just that it was a bit strange, after all this time, the thought of having a stepmum. Cos that's what she would be! And then what about Cass? If Caroline was our stepmum, where would that leave Cass?

"Don't you like her?" said Lottie.

"I do like her! She's really nice. Like, she didn't get mad when Dad reversed into her?" *Or* when she'd sat on my dividers. "Most people would have been absolutely furious."

"My mum would have been," said Lottie. "She nearly got road rage the other day just cos someone cut her up."

"Well, this is it," I said. "Dad needs someone that'll put up with him. You know how hopeless he is."

Lottie giggled. "Like that time he was going round with his glasses on top of his head, complaining he didn't know where he'd put them? And that other time he took us to the shopping centre and forgot where he'd parked the car and we all had to walk round for ages looking for it?"

Lottie and I have been friends ever since Year Three. We were in Year Seven now. She knew Dad pretty well.

"So will you be happy," said Lottie, "if they get married?"

I said, "Yes, cos Dad will be."

"What about that other person?" said Lottie. "The one you used to think he'd marry."

I said, "Polly."

Polly was lovely! And she knew all about history, same as Dad. She was actually a bit like Dad, in some ways. Hugely clever, but not very practical. We'd had loads of fun with Polly! She'd even come with us on holiday once or twice. Cass always used to say that she and Dad were made for each other.

"What happened?" said Lottie. "Has he gone off her?"

"No! It's just that he's known her so long. She's like an old slipper. Sort of… *comfortable*." That was what Cass had said. She said the moment had come and gone. "And now he's met Caroline and she's just, like, really cool! Like a model or something? She even has these shoes that are by that designer man!"

"What designer man?"

"One that makes these really expensive shoes?" Not being into fashion I couldn't immediately think what his name was, but Cass had been well impressed. "Must have cost a fortune," she'd said.

"Sounds a bit posh for your dad," said Lottie.

"She's not posh," I said. "Just super-cool!"

"H'm." Lottie hooked her arm through mine as we wandered back into school at the end of break. "You know what'd be really neat? If your dad could marry my auntie!"

She'd said that before. I never quite liked to tell her that it wouldn't work.

"My auntie's cool," urged Lottie.

"Yes," I said, "I know."

Lottie's auntie is very small and fluffy and dresses like a teenager. She *looks* like a teenager. She is into dancing and karaoke, and going down the pub, which wouldn't suit Dad *at all.* He is very much a stay-at-home-with-his-books sort of person. I don't think Lottie's aunties ever read books. Polly read loads! She and Dad were always lending books to each other and having these long discussions. Now he would be doing it with Caroline. At least, I supposed he would. I didn't know what Dad and Caroline talked about when they were alone together.

"Thing is," I said, "it's a bit too late now." For Dad and Polly, was what I actually meant. Not for Dad and Lottie's auntie. "He's gone all *moonstruck.*"

"What's that mean?" said Lottie.

"It's what Cass says. She says he's like a young boy falling in love for the first time."

"Aw!" Lottie made a gurgling sound. "That's so sweet!"

I supposed that it was. I was genuinely happy for Dad. Caroline was special, and I was really pleased that he had found her. But it is a bit strange, seeing your own dad being all moonstruck.

"When's she moving in?" said Lottie. "Caroline? When's she coming?"

"Not sure. Next month, I think."

"Can I come and meet her?"

I promised that she could.

Lottie giggled. "I can't wait to see what she's like!"

That night, Dad broke the news that Caroline would be coming to live with us the week after next.

"Is that all right?"

Me and Em both nodded, eager to reassure.

"You really don't mind?"

"Dad!" I looked at him reproachfully. "We just want you to be happy."

"Well, but I want *you* to be happy," said Dad.

"We'll be happy," said Em.

"Yes, cos we *like* Caroline," I said. "We do," I said, "don't we?"

"We do," said Em. "We think she's good for you."

Dad laughed. "Well, I'm glad about that! Anyway, the thing is… it means that Cass will be moving on."

Moving *on*? I felt my jaw drop. How could Cass be moving on?

It was Em, in a small, tight voice who said, "She's not going to be here any more?"

"I realise this has probably come as a bit of a shock," said Dad, "but you know that Cass never planned to stay permanently. It was only ever supposed to be a temporary arrangement, until – well! Until I got back on my feet. I was in a pretty bad way after losing your mum. It was Cass who pulled me through. I never intended her to sacrifice her entire life."

"But, Dad," cried Em, "this is her home! Where is she going to go?"

"She's decided to move in with Becky."

*Cass?* Moving in with Becky? It's true that Cass and Becky have been friends since uni, but how could she bear to just go off and leave us?

"Be fair," said Dad. "I realise this must be upsetting

for you both, but try to see it from Cass's point of view. Apart from anything else, think how much more convenient it'll be for her. Do away with all that travelling."

"It's not that far!" protested Em.

Cass and Becky run an arts and crafts shop in Lewes. It really *isn't* that far. Not from Brighton.

"Sweetheart, it's her choice," said Dad. "We mustn't be selfish about it. Cass does have her own life to lead."

"But this is her life. With us!"

"Look at it this way," said Dad. "When you grow up you're going to want to leave home, aren't you? Have a place of your own. Do your own thing. It's the same for Cass. All those years ago she gave up her independence to come and take care of us. Now it's time for her to move on. You probably don't know this, but before your mum died Cass had great plans. She and Becky had just left uni. They always intended to set up in business together and share a home. Well, at last they'll be able to. We can't expect Cass to baby us for ever. In any case, we'll have Caroline."

Em fell silent. We both sat there, staring at Dad. I'd only been two years old when Mum died, so I couldn't really remember a time when Cass hadn't lived with us. I'd never stopped to think that maybe she had once had plans of her own. Plans that didn't include *us*.

"We'll still be a family," said Dad. "Caroline's really excited about it. She can't wait to start being a stepmum! She's also just a tiny bit anxious. I've promised her you'll make her feel welcome. I can rely on you, can't I?"

Em cried, "Dad, of course you can!"

"How about Bitsy? Is she OK with it?"

"She'd better be," said Em.

"I am!" I said it indignantly. I could be relied on just as much as Em. I might be sad about Cass leaving us, but I was really looking forward to Caroline moving in. *And* having a super-cool stepmum!

"It'll all work out just fine," said Dad. "You'll see!"

Dad had told us that Cass herself had made the decision to move out. It was her choice! We mustn't be selfish. We tried really hard, but when it came to the point we so didn't want her to go!

"I can't believe," said Em, "that she really wants to."

"Then why is she doing it?" I wailed. Why couldn't we just carry on as we were?

"Oh, Bits, that would never work," said Cass, when we asked her. "You can't have two women in the same house."

"But you and Becky will be," I said.

"That's different," said Cass. "We're friends. We've known each other for ever. Caroline and I have only just met."

"Do you think you'd quarrel?" said Em.

"I'm afraid we might. We're very different from one

another. I doubt if Caroline could tolerate my slapdash ways."

Me and Em fell silent.

"Cheer up!" said Cass. She held out her arms. "Come and have a hug!"

We flung ourselves at her, like we used to do when we were little.

"Do you really *want* to go?" I said.

"I feel sad in lots of ways," said Cass, "but Becky and I have always had these plans, and she's waited very patiently. Besides, it's only right your dad and Caroline should be on their own. And honestly, it's not the end of the world! You can jump on a train and come to visit any time you like. You could even come for the odd weekend. We'll always be there, you'll always be welcome."

I heaved a quivering sigh. "It won't be the same," I said.

"No, it won't," agreed Cass. "And at first I expect it will all seem a bit strange. But we'll get used to it!

It's what happens in life – things change. And look at it this way – it means you'll have a second home! *And* one of you can take over my room. How about that? Bitsy? You're always complaining you haven't got enough space for all your things."

It was true, my little room over the garage was hardly any bigger than a cupboard. But I refused to be comforted! I'd be willing to sleep in a tent if it meant Cass could stay.

"Suppose Dad was going to marry Polly?" said Em. "Would you still have to go?"

Cass laughed. "Yes, I would! Married people need their space."

"Even if it was Polly?"

"Even if it was Polly, which I know we once thought it was going to be, but Caroline is your dad's choice. She's the one he wants to spend the rest of his life with, and I need you two girls to promise me you'll do your very best to make things work. For your dad's sake! It won't all be plain sailing, I'm not pretending that it will. You're used to me and my sloppy ways, but Caroline's a businesswoman. She has no idea what it's like living with two stroppy kids."

"Stroppy?" I was indignant. "We're not stroppy!"

"You think not?" said Cass. "Em mightn't be, but you… you can be a little monster!"

"I'll make sure she behaves," promised Em.

"I'll *behave*," I said. "You don't have to get all bossy about it."

I wanted Dad to be happy just as much as she did.

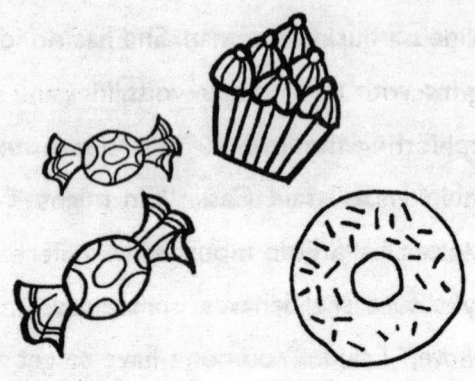

# CHAPTER FOUR

Cass moved out on Saturday morning. Becky came to help her, with Dad hovering anxiously in the background, asking if there was anything he could do, while me and Em carried stuff out to the car and tried not to let our feelings get the better of us. I didn't actually cry, cos I don't do crying. If I'd been the sort of person that did, then I expect I probably would have, but as I'm not, I didn't. I don't care what Em said! She was just trying to cover up for her own sniffles and snuffles. I saw her blotting her eyes on her sleeve when she didn't know I was watching. *She* said it was an allergy (she has lots of allergies) but I knew different. Cass and Becky obviously did too, cos they gave us both a big cuddle and told us to remember that we would always be welcome.

"We'll keep the spare bed made up specially for you!"

When Becky and Cass had driven off, Dad said he was going round to Caroline's to help her pack the last of her stuff ready for tomorrow.

"We'll come by and pick you up at about six, OK?"

Me and Em nodded rather glumly. We were all going out for a pizza, which normally we'd have looked forward to.

"What are you planning to do while I'm out?" said Dad.

"Haven't really thought about it," I said.

"I don't suppose…" Dad made the suggestion rather nervously, without a great deal of hope. "I don't suppose you could have a little tidy?"

"We could do that," said Em. She trod somewhat viciously on my toe. I glared at her. What was that for? I wasn't going to say anything!

"Bless you!" Dad gave us both a quick hug. "You're stars! I'll see you later."

Dad went off, leaving me and Em standing there.

"It's only fair," said Em. "We have to do *something* to earn our pocket money."

"Didn't say we didn't," I said.

"So let's get on with it."

After slogging all round the house, flicking at dust and sucking up crowds of cat fur, we went upstairs to start transferring things from my little room to what had been Cass's room.

"This ought to cheer you up," said Em.

"Who says I need cheering up?" I said.

That was when she claimed she'd seen me cry.

"*I* didn't cry," I said. "You did!"

"I did not!" said Em. "That was my allergy."

We argued for a bit, in a pointless kind of fashion, with me saying it wasn't and Em saying it was, but our hearts weren't really in it.

"Let's go and see if we can find something for lunch," said Em.

We trailed back downstairs to look in the fridge and see what there was.

I said, "Eggs?"

"If you like," said Em.

"Scrambled?"

"Whatever."

"You do the toast," I said. "I'll do the eggs."

"Just don't make them all sloppy. I hate it when they're sloppy."

I said, "Yes, and I hate it when they're like rubber." Em is useless at cooking. When she does scrambled eggs you can almost string them across the room like a piece of elastic. The truth is, Em is not really much interested in food. Unlike me! I am definitely a bit of a foodie. But I didn't want to quarrel with her. Not today. I cooked the eggs until they were practically solid and slapped them down on to the toast, which, typically, she had managed to burn. I kept quiet as a mouse.

"This is how I like it," said Em. "Not all slippy and slimy."

Honestly! You could never take her to a high class restaurant; you would just absolutely cringe.

"Do you really think Dad and Caroline will get married?" I said, as I prodded at my overdone egg.

"Cass thinks so," said Em. "She says the only time she's ever seen Dad so in love was when he was dating Mum. And Caroline obviously loves *him* or she wouldn't be moving in. Cass reckons there'll be a spring wedding. That'll be fun!"

I said, "Not sure I'd marry Dad if I was Caroline."

"What?" Em looked at me sharply. "Why not?"

I said, "*Pratt?*"

Whoever would want to change from being Caroline Scott-Mason to Caroline Pratt? Not me!

"That's just stupid," said Em. "People in love don't care about that sort of thing."

"I would," I said. "When I get married it's going to be to someone with a really romantic kind of name." Valentine, for instance. That was my current favourite. Flora Valentine!

Em sniffed. "You are just *so* pathetic."

"Names are important," I said.

"Only to really shallow sorts of people. Caroline's not shallow."

I said, "Nor am I, but suppose I get to be famous at something? I wouldn't want to be known as Flora Pratt!"

"Omigod," said Em, "you're even more shallow than I thought! Anyway, what would you ever be famous for?"

"I could be famous," I said.

Em said, "Yes, and pigs might fly! You are *so* ridiculous at times."

I sulked for a bit, but I can never keep up a sulk for very long. My mouth just seems to open of its own accord and things come blurting out.

"I always thought Dad would marry Polly!"

"Well, he's marrying Caroline," said Em. "And you ought to be happy for him!"

"I am," I said.

"Then why go on about Polly?"

"I'm not going on!" I pushed my plate away. "This egg is horrible! *And* you burnt the toast."

"Don't change the subject," said Em. "I want to know what your problem is."

"Haven't got a problem!"

"Then why did you mention her?"

"*I* don't know!"

I would have told her if I could, but I didn't understand it myself. I didn't have anything against Caroline. I was proud that Dad had found such a cool girlfriend. Tonight we'd go for a pizza and I just bet heads would turn to look at us. They wouldn't ever turn to look at Polly. Or any of the rest of us. Just Caroline. Cos she was so smart and so together. She was my role model!

"Fact is," said Em, "you can't dictate who people are going to fall in love with. Dad's in love with Caroline, and that's all that matters."

Fiercely I said, "Yes, and I'm glad – and I'm glad they're going to get married! I'm looking forward to it." I was! I really was. "Next time," I said, "I'm going to do the eggs the way *I* like them."

Em hunched a shoulder. "Whatever," she said.

Now that Caroline was living with us we had a whole new set of rules. Well, not rules, exactly. More like suggestions. Things we might want to think about. Caroline said it wasn't her place to turn our routine upside down, *but*…

Maybe it would be better if we did the washing-up

as we went along, rather than letting it mount up on the draining board. Maybe it would be a good idea if we put the ironing in a special ironing basket rather than dumping it in great piles on the table. And how about putting old newspapers in the paper box and not leaving dirty cups and plates all over the place to gather mould?

She wasn't unpleasant about it.

"It's just an idea," she'd say, picking up Em's hockey boots and tossing them into the cupboard under the stairs. "You know what your dad's like – if there was an elephant in the room he'd manage to trip over it. And maybe if we rinsed out cat-food tins before recycling them? What do you think? It's not so bad now, but come summer there'll be flies around. We don't want maggots."

You couldn't really argue with her. As Em said, it all made sense. I wouldn't have argued anyway, cos of promising to behave myself, though I did sort of mention it to Dad, just casually, not, like, complaining or anything.

"Did you know," I said, "Caroline wants us to put everything away so's you don't fall over it?"

Dad said, "A wise precaution. I am a very clumsy person."

"But even the *ironing*," I said. "Nobody could fall over the ironing!"

"I probably could," said Dad.

"But it's on the table!"

"Ah, well, that's clutter," said Dad. "You have to remember, Caroline's not used to living with clutter."

I didn't bother telling him about the cat-food tins and the maggots or any of the other stuff. He'd only say that Caroline wasn't used to living with that sort of thing. I did try mentioning it – just *mentioning* it – to Cass, when I spoke to her on the phone, but she wasn't at all sympathetic. She just laughed and said, "About time too!"

I said, "About time *what*?"

"About time someone imposed a bit of order."

"You never did," I said.

"That was a fault," said Cass, "not a virtue. Learn to live with it! You've had it far too easy for far too long."

Em agreed. She said I wasn't being fair on Caroline.

"She's only trying to keep the place looking nice. When we're left to ourselves it's just a mess. I mean, look at this!"

We were dusting and vacuuming again. We had to do it once a week now. *Once a week!* Caroline said, "It's no use huffing and puffing, Flora! Houses don't clean themselves."

She didn't say it crossly; she never got cross. She just had this huge obsession with things being scrubbed and polished and all put away in their right places.

"*Look!*" Em had pushed back a chair and was pointing rather hysterically, I thought, at something she had discovered underneath it.

I said, "What?"

"*Look!*" shrieked Em.

I looked. "Ugh, yuck!" I said. "Is that cat poo?"

"It's a *fur ball*," said Em. "I thought you were supposed to have vacuumed in here?"

I said, "I have! I did! She must have crept in and done it while my back was turned."

"Excuse me," said Em, "but Bella has been asleep on my bed *all morning*. She obviously did this days ago! It's all dried up."

"So what's the big fuss?" I said. "If it's just a fur ball?"

"The fuss is that you were supposed to have vacuumed!"

"Yes, but I don't move the *furniture*," I said.

"You mean you just go round it? Well!" Em sat back on her heels. "That's the last time you get to do the vacuuming. You can stick to dusting in future!"

Triumphantly I said, "I don't move things when I'm dusting, either, so ha!"

"You're disgusting!" Em was clutching the fur ball in a paper hanky. She thrust it at me. "Go and put it in the bin."

"Why me?" I said.

"Cos you're the one that should have found it!"

Angrily, I snatched it from her. "Anyway," I said, "I'd rather dust than vacuum now we've got proper dusters!"

I only said it to annoy her. We weren't using old bits of rag any more – Caroline said we had to use real dusters. She said rags just moved the dust about from one place to another. The new dusters were bright yellow and soft. Em didn't say anything, but I knew she didn't really approve. She was as bad as Cass. If she had her way we would recycle everything from bits of string to old pairs of knickers. She is fearsomely committed. She says it's all about saving the planet.

"Pish to the planet!" I stalked grandly from the room. I hoped it was grandly. It is not easy to be grand when you are round and short and called Pratt.

Em came storming after me. "What do you mean, *Pish to the planet?* And what kind of stupid word is that, anyway?"

I said, "*Pish*." It was something I'd read in a book about olden times. It had somehow appealed to me. I liked the sound of it. Plus we are always being told at school to broaden our vocabulary.

Em looked at me darkly. "You'll be sorry when we've got global warming going on all over the place."

"What's global warming got to do with dusters?"

"We don't *need* dusters!"

"Caroline says we do. So there!" I yanked open the door of the cupboard under the sink and tossed Bella's fur ball into the bin. I was about to slam the door shut when I saw a familiar-looking garment trailing out of the bag we put the rags in. Bright canary yellow with purple hoops. Dad's football jersey! I dragged it out indignantly. "What's this doing in here?"

Dad doesn't actually play football any more. He had to give it up when he slipped on an ice cube and broke his ankle. It wasn't his fault! Anyone could slip on an ice cube if they didn't realise it was there. You don't expect ice cubes to be lying around in the middle of the kitchen floor. Poor Dad! He was so sad when he had to stop playing. His football jersey was one of his most treasured possessions. He wore it all the time.

"Why's it in with the rags?" I said.

Em giggled. "Cos that's what it is! It's a *rag*."

"But it's Dad's favourite," I said. You don't throw away your favourite clothes just cos they're a bit old and faded. You wait till you grow out of them or till they fall to pieces. "It's got to be a mistake," I said.

I folded it lovingly, ready to give to Dad when he got home. He and Caroline had gone into town to do some shopping. Dad had never gone shopping when Cass was with us, but he seemed to like it with Caroline.

"Dad!" I rushed into the hall as soon as I heard the front door open. "Look what I found!"

"Ah," said Caroline, "the famous football jersey."

"It was in the *rag* bag!"

"Er… yes. Well." Dad shot a sideways glance at Caroline, who laughed as she went through to the kitchen.

"It's all right, you can tell them!"

"Tell us what?" said Em.

Dad cleared his throat. "Caroline thought it had probably reached the end of its natural life."

I said, "Da-a-ad! Your football jersey!"

"I know, I know! It's very sad. But I fear its time has come. Caroline says she can no longer bear to be seen with me when I'm wearing it. As from today," said Dad, "I am a changed man!"

I said, "Changed how?"

"See for yourself." Dad gestured to the bags that he and Caroline had brought in with them.

"Ooh, clothes!" said Em.

"It seems I'm to have a new look." Dad said it sort of half proudly and half bashfully. "You need no longer be ashamed to be seen with me!"

"Dad, we never were," I said.

"Blame it on me," said Caroline, coming back into the room. "I am nothing but a nag and a bully!"

"She is." Dad said it fondly, like he enjoyed being

nagged and bullied. "She complained I looked like a carthorse shambling down the road."

"It wasn't just the clothes," said Caroline. "It was the hair, sticking out all over the place."

"You've had it cut!" said Em.

"*Styled*." Caroline reached up and patted Dad's head. "What do you think?"

"I think it's lovely," said Em.

"Flora?"

"I knew there was something different," I said.

"Yes, but what do you think?"

"Yeah, it's cool," I said.

It just didn't look like Dad.

# CHAPTER FIVE

At half term, as a special treat, Caroline took us up to town one afternoon to see *The Lion King*. Dad couldn't come cos he was working, so it was just me and Em.

We'd never been on our own with Caroline before. It was very different from being with Cass. With Cass you could play around and have a giggle, and she would join in. Caroline was way more serious. And a whole lot stricter! Not that she told us off or anything, but on the train, when she thought I was making too much noise, she put a finger to her lips and went, "Flora! Shhh!" And when we reached London and I went racing ahead to the Underground she called to me quite sharply to come back.

"I don't want to get home with only one of you! Your dad would never forgive me."

Em said, "Dad got home with only one of us, once. He came to pick me up from school and left Bitsy behind in the playground."

"Yes, well," said Caroline, "that's your dad for you, absent-minded professor! I'm a business-woman, I'm supposed to have more sense. So let's all keep together. Please! London's a big place, it's very easy to get lost."

I felt like boasting that I'd been to London loads of times with Cass and that she'd never minded if I skipped ahead or went racing off by myself. But I didn't cos it wouldn't have been polite. Dad had made a big deal about Caroline taking a day off work specially to be with us. He didn't actually *say* that I should make an effort to behave myself, but I knew that was what he meant. People are always telling me to behave myself. I can't understand why. They never tell Em to behave herself. Probably because she tends to keep her feelings all bottled up and everyone thinks she is so good and patient. My feelings just whoosh about all over the place, and so I get this totally undeserved reputation. Even Cass had accused me of being a little monster. But I'm not! I'm really not! I can be just as good and patient as Em if I set my mind to it.

I didn't say a word when Caroline made us stand still on the escalator instead of galloping down, which is what I like to do. I didn't even complain when she insisted I took her hand as we crossed the road, even though it made me feel like I was five years old. She was only trying to be a good stepmum.

"It's such a pity your dad isn't here," she said, as we reached the theatre. "He doesn't know what he's missing!"

I opened my mouth to say that Dad didn't really go for musicals, but immediately shut it again before any words could come blurting out. I absolutely *can* control myself.

As it happened, Caroline was right. Dad really *didn't* know what he was missing! *The Lion King* was without doubt the most brilliant and amazing show I had ever seen. Excitedly, as we left the theatre, I told Caroline that it had to be my A1 favourite musical.

"Of all time. Ever!"

Caroline seemed pleased. She said, "I'm so glad you enjoyed it."

I was glad too. Not just that I'd enjoyed it, but that Caroline was pleased. It's nice when you've made someone happy. She'd made me happy and I'd made her happy!

Dad was waiting to meet us at the station.

"How did it go?" he said. "Did you have a good time?"

I knew he was bracing himself, expecting me to have some kind of grumble, like We couldn't hear properly, We couldn't see properly, I was bored.

"Well?" said Dad. "What's the verdict?"

"Brilliant!" I said. "My favourite musical ever!"

A big beam spread itself across Dad's face. "That is good news," he said.

So now I'd made Dad happy, everyone was happy!

"Let's go and rustle up something for dinner," said Caroline, as we arrived home. "What do you two girls fancy?"

Eagerly I cried, "Egg and chips!"

"Oh, Flora." Caroline looked at me reproachfully. "You've already had a KitKat."

"Only a small one," I pleaded. I'd got hungry on the way home. I had to eat something.

"Is egg and chips what you used to have with Cass?"

"Just once a week," said Em.

We hadn't even had them *once* since Caroline came. Caroline shook her head, as if she couldn't believe anyone would eat egg and chips ever.

"I suppose she let you have those dreadful fattening lemon things for pudding as well?"

Oh! I knew she hadn't liked them.

"We wouldn't have had egg and chips *and* lemon possets," said Em. "Not both at the same time."

"I'm relieved to hear it! I'm just surprised Cass let you have them at all, seeing as she's such a food freak."

Earnestly, Em said, "She's not a freak. Truly! She just doesn't believe in eating animals."

"Yet she didn't mind you stuffing yourselves with chips and cream and sugar. Honestly, Emily, it's so bad for you!"

Em bit her lip. She'd already told me that she didn't like being called Emily; she didn't think it sounded friendly. I was getting quite used to Flora. I liked it! I'd even suggested it to Lottie, only she seemed quite incapable of remembering.

"Let's have something easy," said Caroline. "How about salad?"

Em said, "Yesss!"

Em likes salad. Especially lettuce. How can anybody like lettuce? It doesn't taste of anything. You might just as well chew grass. Em's eating habits are very peculiar. More like those of a rabbit than a human being. She has even been known to eat lettuce sandwiches.

Glumly I watched as she and Caroline started laying out tomatoes and radishes and other hugely exciting bits of vegetable matter. Cucumbers, for example. Yuck! I loathe cucumbers.

"What about afters?" I said.

"Got any suggestions?"

She obviously wouldn't let me make lemon possets. And it wasn't any use looking in the fridge. When Cass had been in charge you could always rely on finding something exciting in there. Little pots of cheesecake, or trifle, or Black Forest gateau. Caroline never bought anything yummy. All I could find was yoghurt. Plain yoghurt. *Low fat.*

"No ideas?" said Caroline, chopping away at a pepper. Peppers are something else I loathe. Peppers and cucumbers and onions. Yuck yuck yuck! "How about we make a fresh fruit salad? You can have your silly pretend cream on it, if you want."

She meant soya cream. I knew she didn't really like soya cream; she thought it was just another of Em's food fads. But it made Em ever so happy!

Dad and Caroline had prawns with their salad. Dad ate meat all the time now. He said that we didn't have to eat it if we didn't want to.

"It's entirely up to you. Nobody's going to force you."

Em said, "But, Dad, you're a vegetarian!"

"Not really," said Dad. "I only did it to keep Cass happy."

"But how can you bear it? It would make me feel sick!"

Poor Em was quite distressed. Even I was a bit shocked.

"Are you sure I can't persuade you?" Caroline speared a prawn on the end of her fork and waggled it in front of us. "Your dad's enjoying them."

Em and I both swivelled our eyes reproachfully in Dad's direction.

"Oh, now don't look at him like that! You'll make him feel guilty," said Caroline, "and that's not fair. After all these years being forced to eat nothing but vegetables!"

"I wouldn't exactly say I was forced," said Dad. "It's just – well!" He grinned hopefully at us. "Anything for a quiet life!"

"Are you saying Cass nagged you?" said Em.

"She wouldn't," I said. "Cass never nagged!"

"That's all you know!" said Dad with a chuckle. But Em didn't smile, and I didn't, either. He was being really disloyal. Cass had always said that it was up to us.

"OK, OK!" Dad looked a bit ashamed of himself. "It's true, she didn't nag, but she was the one who took care of all that side of things so it just seemed... easier somehow."

"Line of least resistance." Caroline nodded. "So how about it?" She waved the fork to and fro, with the prawn wobbling about on the end. If Bella had been there she would have snatched it like a shot and made off, but Bella was shut away in the kitchen. Caroline said a cat on the table was more than she could take. "Just one tiny little bite! Who's going to be brave?"

Em recoiled. You'd have thought there was a live worm wriggling on the end of the fork.

"Oh, come on," said Caroline, "it won't hurt you!"

"It's not that." Em said it apologetically, like she didn't want to sound rude or ungracious. "It's just that we don't eat things that have faces."

Caroline gave one of her tinkling laughs. "Prawns don't have faces!"

Em bit her lip. I rushed to her rescue. "They do," I said. "Honestly! If you look at them… they have little eyes. And whiskers."

"They may have whiskers," said Caroline, "but you can hardly claim they have feelings. All they are is lumps of muscle."

I felt myself waver. It is certainly difficult to think of a prawn as being happy, for instance, or sad.

Em, recovering herself, sat forward again. "Maybe if superior beings came here from another planet, they'd think we were just lumps of muscle that didn't have any feelings."

"They'd soon discover differently," said Caroline. "Just a few tests would show them."

I said, "Yes, cos if they went and stuck forks in us we'd scream. Prawns don't scream."

Em turned on me witheringly. "How do you know? Just because you can't hear them! They could be supersonic, like bats."

"Got you there," said Dad.

"I think we'd know if they were supersonic." Caroline was still holding out her prawn, waving it in front of me. "Flora? Are you quite sure?"

I might as well admit, I was tempted. Just to see what it tasted like. Whether it would be soft and gooey, or hard and crunchy. But Em was giving me this really scorching glare, so I forced myself to shake my head and primly said no thank you.

"Oh well, suit yourself." Caroline popped the prawn into her mouth and chewed. It seemed to me that I could hear it squeak, but I must have been imagining it. The prawn was dead. Dead prawns can't squeak.

"You know, I can't help thinking," said Caroline, "that a bit of meat would do you good. I'm not asking you to gorge! Maybe just a couple of times a week. What do you reckon?"

She glanced across at Dad. Dad shrugged his shoulders. "You're welcome to try and persuade them."

"Emily in particular," said Caroline. "She looks to me as if she might be almost anaemic."

"What's anaemic?" I said.

"Not enough red blood cells."

We all turned to look at Em. She had her head bent over her salad, her hair falling over her face.

"She's always been pale," said Dad.

"Well, but if she could just bring herself to eat a bit of meat now and again, it might actually put some colour in her cheeks. It might even help her hair."

I squirmed on Em's behalf. Em is really sensitive about her hair. It's pure silver and really pretty, but it's also very fine and dead straight so that it either lies totally flat or flies about in wisps. Unlike mine, which is only boring mouse – but as thick as a door mat or one of those carpets where your feet sink in as you walk across them.

"Something else," said Caroline. "She could do with putting on a bit of weight. Unlike little Jelly Baby here."

She leant across and playfully patted my tummy. "You're getting to be quite a roly-poly! It's all those chocolate bars and fattening puds."

I felt my face grow slowly crimson. Em peered at me sympathetically through her curtain of hair. Dad, meanwhile, had burst into song.

"*Emily Pratt would eat no fat,*
*Her sister ate no lean.*
*One was thin as a piece of string,*
*And one was a plump little bean!*"

"Beans aren't plump," I said.

"Jelly beans are," said Dad.

"*Donald.*" Caroline smacked at him reprovingly. "I didn't say Flora was plump. Just in danger of becoming a little podgy. Emily, on the other hand, is definitely too thin. If she put on a bit of weight she could wear more attractive clothes, instead of covering herself up all the time in those frumpy sweaters."

Em by now was positively cringing. I cringed with her.

Em is not only sensitive about her hair, but sensitive generally about the way she looks. She is a very *long* person. Long and skinny. She takes after Dad, whereas I take after our mum. In all Mum's photos she is shown as being quite short and chubby. She is also very pretty, which I would like to think I am too, but as nobody has ever mentioned it, I have to accept that I probably am not. The best thing people ever say about me is that I have a cheeky face. I suppose that is meant as a compliment.

"What we have to watch out for," said Caroline, "is that she doesn't become anorexic."

"Anorexic?" Dad was starting to sound alarmed. "You're not getting anorexic, are you, Em? I mean, Emily?"

Em didn't say anything, just bent her head back over her plate. I leapt to her defence.

"She's just a naturally thin kind of person! She's always been a thin kind of person."

"Like you've always been a plumpkin," said Dad

fondly. "It's just the way they're made," he told Caroline. "I don't think there's any problem."

Caroline shook her head. "I'm not saying there is. I'm just saying, Emily could do with filling out a bit. And little Jelly Baby could do with fewer chocolate bars! That's all."

I tried talking about it to Em later. I just wanted to show that I felt for her. I said, "It's not fair Caroline telling you you're too thin. She's every bit as skinny as you are. And *you* eat lemon possets, which is more than she does. She doesn't eat anything at all, hardly."

"She eats meat," said Em. "She thinks it's good for you. Lots of people do."

I said, "Cass didn't."

"Cass was different," said Em. "You can't keep going on about Cass all the time. You've got to learn to accept things the way they are. Caroline's trying really hard."

"Yes," I said. "I know."

"She didn't *have* to take us up to town."

"I know," I said. "I know!"

"*And* she bought the best seats."

"I *know.*"

"*And* she had to take time off work."

"I know, I know!"

"So why are you having a go at her?"

"Cos she was having a go at you! Saying about your hair and everything."

Two spots of colour appeared in Em's cheeks. "She was just trying to show that she cares."

Like saying I was a jelly baby. And Dad agreeing!

I was still brooding about it at bedtime when Em came into my room and rather shyly said, "Look what Caroline's given me."

"What?"

"It's this special treatment that makes your hair thick. She says she's tried it on hers and it really works. I looked it up on the internet," said Em. "It's

ever so expensive! So don't you think that's nice of
her?"

I did, cos it was. She was a really nice person! And
we'd had *such* a good day. I was just so pleased it
had ended happily.

# CHAPTER SIX

When we got back to school after half term I told Lottie about Caroline taking us up to town to see *The Lion King*.

"I'm going to see that," said Lottie. "On my birthday! Mum's promised."

"I hope she's already got tickets," I said, "cos they're

really hard to get. Caroline booked ours *weeks* ago." She had obviously done it right back when she first moved in. All that time she'd been planning it as a special treat! "We were ever so close to the stage," I said. "I've never sat that close before. It must have cost stacks of money."

I wasn't boasting! I just wanted Lottie to know how lovely Caroline would be.

"And then she gave Em some special stuff for her hair," I said, "to stop it being all limp and floppy. That cost stacks of money too! Em looked it up on the internet."

"Does it work?" said Lottie.

"Dunno yet. She hasn't used it." Caroline had said that it worked, but Caroline's hair wasn't as thin as Em's, plus she wore it all piled up in a kind of parcel thing on top of her head, which made it difficult to tell. "Anyway," I said, "it's the thought that counts."

"Sounds as though you're getting on really well," said Lottie. "In spite of all the cleaning and stuff. My mum says having to do housework must have come as a rude shock."

*Oh?* What did Lottie's mum know about it?

"She always says your house looks like a hurricane has gone through it."

What cheek! "For your information," I said, "Cass reckons housework is a boring waste of time. And so do I, if you want to know! I only do it to make Caroline happy."

"What would she do if you said you weren't going to?" said Lottie. And then, answering her own question, "She'd probably complain to your dad. What would your dad do? Would he take her side or yours?" Before I could say anything, she'd gone and answered herself yet again. "I bet he'd take hers! They always do."

What *was* she on about?

I said, "Who?"

"Dads." Lottie said it bitterly. "They always side with mums."

Ah ha! I could guess what had happened here. Lottie had obviously done something to upset her mum, and her mum had gone to her dad, and her dad had taken her mum's side and Lottie was feeling aggrieved. But, as I pointed out, Caroline wasn't our mum.

"She will be," said Lottie. "Soon as they get married."

"Not our real mum," I said. "Only our stepmum."

"Comes to the same thing."

It did not! How could anyone say that a stepmum was the same as a real mum?

"What I mean," said Lottie, "is she'll still be the one your dad sides with. I bet he sides with her right now! I bet if you said you weren't going to do any vacuuming or dusting or washing-up cos you reckoned it was a waste of time, I bet he'd say you'd got to."

Rather coldly I said, "So what?"

"Nothing! I'm just saying."

"So what is your point?"

"There isn't any point. It's just a conversation."

"About what? *Exactly?*"

"About Caroline!" Lottie plunged her arm through mine. "When am I going to see her? I'm dying to see her!"

"She'll be coming next week," I said. "You can see her then."

Next week we had Parents' Evening for Year Seven. Caroline had asked me whether I'd mind if she came with Dad.

"I'd love to see your school and meet some of your teachers. But if you'd rather I didn't, I'll understand."

Dad had said, "Of course you must come! You're part of the family."

It hadn't occurred to me that Caroline would be interested. Truth to tell, I felt quite flattered.

"Bits?" Dad had looked at me rather anxiously. "You don't mind if Caroline comes, do you?"

I said, "No! I'd like her to."

I could see immediately that Dad was pleased. He was really eager for me and Em to get on with Caroline. Specially me. He didn't worry so much about Em. She wasn't likely to play up or go into a sulk or get all stroppy and resentful. Well, and neither was I! Dad didn't realise that Caroline was my role model. Apart from anything else, I wanted to show her off to Lottie! And to the rest of my year.

Back in juniors they'd only ever seen Cass, and however much I loved Cass I had to admit she wasn't the coolest person on earth. At home she mostly wore jeans and sweat shirts, which was what suited her best. But when she went out, like to parents' evenings, she would feel she had to make an effort and look smart. Unfortunately, like Dad, Cass didn't have much dress sense. Her idea of looking smart was long shapeless skirts and woolly tops, usually hand-knitted.

Em would say it was pathetic and small-minded to care about such things, and I never really did until

Caroline came into our lives. Caroline just had this most amazing effect on people. It was like she was some kind of mini celeb. As soon as we walked into the assembly hall on Parents' Evening I could feel people swivelling round to look at us. I saw Peony James's eyes nearly fall out of her head, like, *Who is THAT?* I saw her turn and nudge Zena Walker, and Zena's head snap round and her jaw fall open. It made me feel so good! I didn't care if it was small-minded.

Peony James and Zena Walker are these two really obnoxious people in my class. Think they're the cat's whiskers and the rest of us are just, like, piles of vomit under their feet. They were used to me turning up with Dad looking all shaggy, like a walking haystack, and Cass in her shapeless skirts. Thanks to Caroline, Dad now looked almost smart. Not *totally* smart cos he is quite a shambling sort of person, but at least he'd stopped being a haystack. I had to admit, it was an improvement!

As for Caroline, she was by far the smartest person in the whole room. I couldn't help a little surge of satisfaction. My dad's girlfriend! Soon to be my stepmum! And everyone's eyes were just *riveted*.

She was wearing this beautiful suit, deep dark pink, with a white shirt and a pair of her very expensive designer shoes, the sort with spiky heels and pointy toes. She had her hair, which was very black and glossy, piled on top of her head and held in place with a sparkly comb. I honestly couldn't see why she would have needed the special hair-thickening stuff she'd given Em. Her hair looked perfectly thick enough to me. Perhaps she hadn't really used it at all. Perhaps that was just what she'd told Em, to help Em feel better about herself. A way of making up for saying she looked as if she didn't have enough red blood cells.

While Dad and Caroline were talking to one of the teachers, Lottie came whizzing across the hall. She hissed in my ear.

"*Is that her?*"

I told her that it was. Lottie said, "*Wow.*" A great warm gush of pride came flooding over me.

Lottie went scudding back across the hall to her mum and dad. Her mum looked up and saw me and waved. I waved back. I was almost, like, *bursting.*

"Hey!" Someone was poking me in the ribs. Peony James. "Who's that?" she said. "With your dad?"

Trying to sound offhand I said, "That's Caroline. My dad's girlfriend."

"Is she a model?"

I was tempted to say yes, but you never know when a lie is going to come back and bite you, so I said no, she ran an employment agency.

"Cool!" said Peony.

In the car on the way home Caroline said, "Who was the girl who came over and spoke to you?"

"That was Lottie," I said. "She's my best friend."

"Extraordinarily pretty," said Caroline.

I blinked. Excuse me? She was talking about *Lottie*? Lots is my best friend ever and I would dive into an icy pond to rescue her from drowning without so much as a second thought, but I honestly wouldn't have said she was pretty. Not even just a little bit. Certainly not *extraordinarily* so.

"Give it a couple of years," said Caroline, "the boys won't be able to keep away from her!"

I wondered whether I should pass this on to Lottie. I thought that maybe I might. If I were feeling generous. *If* she behaved herself. I could do without any more of that stepmums-are-the-same-as-real-mums rubbish. On the other hand, would it be good for her? I didn't fancy a best friend that was all vain and puffed up. That would be most tiresome.

"How about the other one?" said Caroline. "The one that rushed over and squeaked at you and went rushing off again. Little gnome-like one?"

*Oh.* Dad chuckled, and even I had to stop myself giggling. Lottie does look a bit like a gnome. She is very short and stubby, even shorter and stubbier than I am, with a little round face and big pouchy cheeks.

"Is she another of your friends?" said Caroline.

I said, "That was Lottie. She's the one I thought you meant."

"Oh!" Caroline sounded amused. "So who was the pretty one?"

In tones of deep loathing I said, "That was Peony James."

"I take it she's *not* a friend?"

I said, "No way!"

"Lottie and B— I mean Flora! Flora!" Dad tapped himself sharply on the side of the head. Just as well he wasn't driving; though mostly, these days, Caroline didn't let him. "Lottie and Flora go way back. They've known each other since Reception."

"In that case, why don't you ask her over?" said Caroline. "How about this Friday? She could spend the night, if you like. Have a sleepover. Isn't that what you call them? Sleepovers?"

"They don't sleep," said Dad. "They stay awake all night yattering."

"That's all right," said Caroline. "They can yatter. How about Emily? Does she have anyone she'd like to invite?"

"Does she?" As usual, Dad had to turn to me for an answer. He really doesn't know *what* is going on around him.

I said, "Don't you remember? Her friend Janis isn't there any more. She left last term." Cass would have known.

"So who is she friends with now?"

"Not sure," I said.

Dad sighed. "It's so hard to keep up with them."

"What about boys?" said Caroline. "Does she not have a boyfriend?"

She made it sound like there was something wrong if you didn't have a boyfriend by the time you were Em's age.

"She's only thirteen," I said.

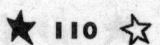

"I'm sure your friend Peony will have started long before then!"

Stolidly I said, "She's *not* my friend."

"Sorry, sorry!" Caroline threw up her hands. "I forgot."

"Em does *know* boys," I said. "I just don't know whether she's got an actual boyfriend. She could have. She doesn't tell me *everything*."

Dad said, "She doesn't tell me anything."

She used to tell Cass. Em and Cass were really close.

Dad shook his head. "She's always been the secretive sort. Hugs things to herself."

"Unlike little Jelly Baby here." Caroline laughed. "She's no shrinking violet, are you?"

"Oh, Bitsy's never been backward in coming forward," said Dad.

"You mean Flora," said Caroline.

*Yes*, I thought. *Flora*. Not Jelly Baby! I knew Caroline was only teasing, so I tried not to mind, though I can't

imagine anyone actually *wanting* to be called Jelly Baby, even just in fun.

"Anyway," said Caroline, "don't forget to ask Lottie about Friday."

"I'll text her," I said. "She's bound to say yes cos she's dying to meet you!"

Lottie didn't just say yes, she called me straight back and shrieked, "Yay! At last!"

I told her that I didn't know what she was getting so excited about. "It's only Caroline," I said.

Only my role model! I couldn't help feeling a glow of pride.

At lunch next day Lottie couldn't stop talking about it.

"I pointed her out to my mum. Mum thinks she looks dead classy! She said she wouldn't have thought your dad would be her type. She always says your dad looks like a mad professor! Like he's been dragged through a hedge backwards. Mum almost didn't

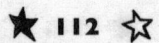

recognise him," gushed Lottie. "She said, 'Oh look, Bitsy's dad is wearing a suit. Doesn't he look nice!' I told her it was Caroline, buying him new clothes and everything. Why are you eating lettuce leaves, by the way?"

"Fancied them," I said.

"You're not trying to *lose weight*?" said Lottie.

What if I was? She didn't have to comment. Lottie may be my very best friend, but she does have this tendency to *niggle*.

"*Are you*?" she said.

I was saved from having to reply by the sudden appearance of Peony and Zena, on their way to join the lunch queue.

"Hey!" Peony stopped. "You know those shoes your dad's girlfriend was wearing? Were they Jimmy Choo?"

"No idea," I said.

"I think they were!"

"They were." Zena nodded.

"Cool!" said Peony.

She was looking at me with new respect. I couldn't help feeling just the tiniest little bit flattered. When had the great Peony James ever condescended to take any notice of me? I knew I was being shallow, and that Em would be ashamed of me, but just now and again it is nice to bask in reflected glory. I think that is what it's called.

Peony and Zena went on their way.

"Idiots," said Lottie.

"Complete morons," I said.

"My mum would have noticed if they were Jimmy Choos."

"Whoever's they were," I said, "they were really expensive."

"Yeah, well, if they were Jimmy Choos, they would be."

Lottie speared a chunk of chicken. I watched greedily as she popped it in her mouth. Lettuce is *so* boring. Was I really a jelly baby? I squinted down at my tummy, trying to see if it wobbled.

"What are you doing?" said Lottie. She speared another piece of chicken. I followed it as it went into her mouth.

"D'you think I could have a taste?" I said.

Lottie's eyes grew round. "You want some chicken?"

"I just want to see what it's like."

"I thought you weren't allowed."

"I can if I want! It's my choice. I just want to *try* it."

Doubtfully, as if she were committing some criminal act, Lottie propelled a chunk towards my mouth. "Open!"

Obediently, I did so.

"Chew!"

I chewed. I'm not really sure what I was expecting. It wasn't like anything I'd ever had before.

"So what d'you reckon?" said Lottie.

I swallowed. "It tastes sort of... weird."

"Don't you like it?"

I wrinkled my nose. "I'm not sure."

"I expect you have to get used to it," said Lottie. "Like avocado. I hated avocado the first time I had it. I thought it was like eating a bar of soap. It's probably the same with meat."

"Caroline reckons we ought to have it at least once a week. She says Em should, specially, cos of looking like she's not got enough red blood cells."

"My mum's always said that," said Lottie. "She says if Em was her daughter she'd make sure she ate properly."

I thought to myself that if Caroline couldn't persuade Em to change her eating habits, there wasn't much chance of Lottie's mum being able to. Em can be unbelievably stubborn. It is what's called *sticking to your principles*. I have principles! I just don't always stick to them.

"Know what some people do?" said Lottie. "They eat insects. They cover them in chocolate and they crunch them up. I don't know whether they eat them alive or whether they're dead. I d—"

"Do you mind?" I said. "That's disgusting."

"These things happen," said Lottie.

I said, "Loads of things happen. You don't have to *talk* about them."

Lottie cackled. "You're just feeling guilty cos you ate some of my chicken!"

It is really annoying how just now and again Lottie manages to be right.

# CHAPTER SEVEN

I was quite surprised when I got back on Friday afternoon with Lottie to find the table all laid for a proper sit-down tea. I was more used to just grabbing stuff from the fridge and rushing off upstairs with it. Cass always said, "Help yourselves! Whatever you fancy." I wasn't sure about sitting down at the table.

I didn't say anything, though, cos it wouldn't have been polite – not when Caroline had gone to so much trouble.

She was there to greet us, like a mum out of a book. The sort of mum you read about, smiling as you come through the door. Cass would more likely have been out digging the garden, or watering her pot plants. Caroline was making a real effort! I decided that I would make one too.

"This is Lottie," I said.

Caroline said, "Hello, Lottie! I'm Caroline."

She held out her hand. Lottie immediately turned bright pink, like she wasn't quite sure what she was supposed to do. Like perhaps she ought to curtsey. In the end she poked out a grubby paw, all covered in blue biro. Caroline laughed.

"It looks as though you've got a leaky pen!"

That just about did it for Lottie; even the tips of her ears were now pink. She is very easily impressed, though in fairness I have to admit that Caroline was

looking extra specially cool. She was only wearing jeans and a shirt, but even I could see that the jeans were like some kind of designer label. The shirt probably was as well. Nothing Caroline wore was ever ordinary. I could see why Peony had thought she might be a model.

"OK, girls!" Caroline gestured towards the table. "Tea's all ready. Emily!" She turned and called up the stairs. "Time for tea!"

"Oh," I said, "is Em joining us?"

"Of course she is! I thought for once it would be nice if we could all sit down together. Even your dad said he'd try to get back in time, if he can. I do think family meals are important! How about you, Lottie? Do you sit down as a family?"

Lottie looked like she had gone into some kind of trance. I poked her.

"*Well?*" I said. "*Do you?*"

Lottie jumped. "Oh! Yes. We always eat together. Mum insists."

"Good for her," said Caroline.

I looked at Lottie with narrowed eyes. I simply didn't believe it! Lottie's dad is a long-distance lorry driver and hardly ever there for normal mealtimes, and her brother Charlie is away at uni. She was just cosying up to Caroline!

Em came downstairs cradling Bella in her arms. Caroline said, "Emily! Cat outside, please?" She said it very nicely, like she always said everything, but somehow you just knew she expected to be obeyed. I guess it was because of being boss at her employment agency.

Em kissed Bella on top of her head. She said, "Good girl! You wait in the kitchen. I won't be long."

"Honestly," said Caroline, "you'd think I was asking you to throw her out of the house! We don't have cats in here while we're eating," she told Lottie. "Not when they keep jumping on the table and helping themselves to food."

"No," said Lottie, sounding very earnest. "My mum always said that wasn't healthy."

"She's absolutely right," said Caroline.

Lottie beamed and looked smug. She'd really got it bad!

Dad arrived just as we were sitting down.

"Ah, tea," he said. "Lovely! What have we got? Good evening, Lottie, by the way."

"Dad, it's afternoon," I said.

"Is it?" said Dad. "Well, I never! So it is."

Lottie giggled. She and Dad were old friends.

"What's this?" he said. "Sausage rolls?"

Cass used to do sausage rolls. *Mock* sausage. I said, "Yum!" and reached out for one, thinking how nice it was of Caroline to go to such trouble. She'd not only got sausage rolls, but lots of little pudding things. Trifle and chocolate and creamy fruit fools. All the kinds of stuff she normally didn't approve of.

Confidently I bit into my sausage roll. I knew at once that it didn't taste right. This wasn't the sort of sausage roll that Cass made! I stared round, wild-eyed, wondering what to do.

"What is it?" said Em. "What's the matter?"

I gulped, and then swallowed. I couldn't help it! It was like a sort of reflex action.

"It's not meat?" said Em. "You haven't eaten meat?"

I nodded convulsively. Em said, "*Bitsy!*"

"Oh, God, I forgot," said Caroline. "I was going to do some egg and cress sandwiches for you. Emily—"

"You've *swallowed* it," said Em.

Guiltily I put the sausage roll down before I could be tempted to take another bite.

"Emily, I'm so sorry," said Caroline, "but do you think you could just try it? For me? Please?"

She hadn't really forgotten to do the sandwiches, she'd been hoping she could tempt Em into eating meat. I knew she had Em's best interests at heart, but I could have told her it would never work.

Caroline heaved a sigh. "You'd better go and find yourself something else."

Em, pale-faced, left the room. I didn't know whether to follow her or not.

"You might as well finish that sausage roll now you've started," said Caroline.

I only did it cos it would have been rude not to. And cos Em wasn't there to see. Caroline shook her head.

"Donald, I'm really worried about Emily. She's far too thin; she looks like a ghost."

Lottie, with her mouth full of sausage roll, said, "My mum's never thought it's right, forcing children to be vegetarian."

"Well, to be fair," said Dad, "no one's ever forced her, but I do agree she looks a bit anaemic."

"If she'd just *try* it," said Caroline. "Flora's eating it! She doesn't seem to have a problem."

I nibbled furtively. Dad said, "No, well, Flora... she's my little Jelly Baby. She'd eat anything!"

With a sly look at me across the table Lottie said, "She ate some of my chicken at lunch today."

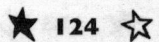

I kicked out at her furiously. Why did she have to go and mention that? She said afterwards that she thought it would be all right since Em was out of the room. But Caroline immediately latched on to it.

"Well, there you are then! Maybe *you* could talk to her, Flora?"

I said, "Me? Talk to Em?"

"Why not? You're her sister! She's more likely to listen to you."

She was more likely to throw something at me. Well, no, she wouldn't do that – she is not at all a violent sort of person. She would just give me this look, all sad and reproachful, like, *Bitsy, how could you?*

"Apart from anything else," said Caroline, "it would make catering so much easier if we all ate the same things. And now that you've broken the ice, so to speak..." She pushed the plate of sausage rolls towards me. I hesitated, just for a moment, but then

I thought of Em in the kitchen, searching for food that wasn't dead animal, and I felt like the worst kind of traitor.

"Oh, Flora," said Caroline, "don't let Emily intimidate you!"

"She doesn't," I said. I suddenly felt very loyal towards my sister. "I feel exactly the same way she does."

"I'm afraid it's what they've got used to," said Dad. "You'll have to be patient."

On Saturday, after Lottie had gone home, me and Em were going to Lewes to stay overnight with Becky and Cass. Caroline had offered to drive us, but at the last minute Em decided we ought to go by ourselves, on the train.

"Cos it's so much greener."

Caroline pulled a face, like, *Pardon me for offering!* "Do I take it your aunt Cass goes everywhere by train?"

Em said, "Only when it's too far for her to cycle."

"Oh my," said Caroline. "How can one ever hope to compete?"

Dad put his arm round her. He gave her a bit of a squeeze and said, "Don't be daft! You don't have to."

"I couldn't anyway," said Caroline. "What with eating meat and poisoning the planet with noxious fumes and—"

"Maybe you could get an electric car?" I said. "That wouldn't be so bad."

"Or you could try cycling," said Em. She said it quite seriously. Em is always serious when it comes to the environment. She wasn't being rude or anything. But this sort of *look* passed across Caroline's face, like she thought Em was deliberately having a go at her.

Dad chuckled. "I can't see Caroline on a bicycle!"

"No, and *you* certainly shouldn't be allowed on one," said Caroline. "You'd be flying over the handlebars every five minutes. Not to mention running down pedestrians!"

We all laughed at that, even Em. But somehow I just had this feeling Caroline hadn't really been joking. She didn't seem to like it much when me and Em talked about Cass.

Dad insisted on coming to the station to see us off. We walked there, feeling very virtuous.

"Do I get a gold star?" said Dad.

Em said, "*Dad!* Me and Bitsy walk further than this to school every day."

"I suppose you do," said Dad in tones of some wonderment, like he'd never even thought about it before. "Well, give us a call if you want us to come and pick you up. I'm not sure how good the trains are on a Sunday."

Rather fiercely, as we waved goodbye to Dad, Em hissed, "I'd sooner *walk* back than ask for a lift!"

We'd been counting the days till we could see Cass again. She was waiting for us on the platform at Lewes, a familiar figure in jeans and an old parka. I shrieked, "Cass!"

Cass held out her arms and we ran into them. I hugged her just as hard as I could. "We've missed you so much!"

It was lovely being with Cass again, but a bit sad as well, cos already she seemed to belong more to Becky than she did to us. I had this feeling that even if Dad were to ask her to come back, she wouldn't really want to. We just weren't part of her everyday life any more.

On Sunday, after lunch, both Cass and Becky walked us back to the station. While Em was striding ahead with Becky, Cass asked me how things were.

"Em seems a bit troubled. Is she all right?"

"Far as I know," I said.

"There's nothing upsetting her?"

I thought about it. "Only Caroline trying to get her to eat meat. She's trying to get us both to eat meat, but specially Em. She says Em hasn't got enough blood cells and that's why she's so pale and if she ate meat her hair would get thicker and she wouldn't be so thin and she could dress better. Or something."

"Ah," Cass nodded. "I'm probably getting the blame for that, aren't I."

"Dad just says that Caroline's got to be patient."

Cass shook her head. "She'll never talk Em into eating meat."

"No, cos Em's got principles," I said. "I've got them too, of course." Just because I'd had a bite of Lottie's chicken and accidentally – and *entirely* by mistake – eaten a sausage roll, didn't mean I hadn't got principles.

"I just hope," said Cass, "she doesn't make herself ill."

"You mean cos of not eating meat?"

"No! Not eating meat doesn't make you ill. I haven't eaten it for almost forty years and I'm doing all right, wouldn't you say?" I nodded. Cass is one of those people that never even catches a cold. "I just hate the thought of Em being bullied."

I assured Cass that Caroline never bullied, she just made suggestions.

"It's cos she worries about us — well, about Em, mainly."

"I worry about her too," said Cass. "She's not like you. You're a tough little cookie!"

"Is that good?" I said.

"Well, it means you can stick up for yourself. It doesn't necessarily mean you're all sweetness and light! What about your dad? What does he have to say?"

I crinkled my forehead. "He doesn't really say anything."

"Typical," said Cass.

"Mostly, on the whole, he agrees with her."

"With Caroline?"

"Well — yes. Most of the time." It was what Lottie had said — dads always sided with mums. Even when they were only stepmums. Even when they wouldn't even be *that* until they were married.

"He thinks Em ought to give in?"

"No, he just thinks she looks a bit –" I waved a hand – "neemic?"

"Anaemic," Cass sighed. "I'm sure she's not. She's just naturally pale-skinned. Oh dear! I wonder if I should have a word with him?"

"You could," I said. "He listens to you."

Cass bit her lip. "I don't know. It might not be wise. I really shouldn't interfere; it's none of my business any more. It's between your dad and Caroline."

We'd almost reached the station.

"I'll tell you what," said Cass. "Just keep an eye on Em for me. Will you do that?"

I nodded.

"And stand by her. You know? She needs your support."

"I always support her," I said. "I'm not going to eat meat any more than she is!"

"Oh, Bitsy, that's not what I meant. What you eat is entirely up to you!"

"But I won't," I said. "I won't!" Even if Caroline *was* my role model.

"Just watch out for your sister," begged Cass.

I didn't see it as odd, Cass asking me to watch out for Em. Em may be cleverer than I am, and of course she is older, but she takes things too much to heart. That is what Cass always says. Em *cares* too much. She is too nice. Unfortunately, it doesn't always pay to be nice. That is the conclusion I have come to. Sometimes I think it is better to be a tough cookie and fight your corner.

Next morning when Em got up she was all wheezing and spluttering. It's how she gets when she is bothered or upset. She sounded like a set of bagpipes coming into the kitchen.

"Oh, my goodness," said Caroline. "What's brought this on?"

I could have told her what had brought it on. It was all the pressure she was under to give in and make people happy. It was people *going on* at her.

"Do you need the doctor?" Caroline hovered, anxiously. "Shall I call him?"

"It's all right," said Dad, "she's just a bit allergic. Aren't you, kiddo?"

Dad ruffled Em's hair. He has never learnt that Em hates it when people do that. She takes ages trying to arrange her hair so that it looks good. Just the least little pat, or even a puff of wind, can then go and mess it all up. But Dad has hair like straw, so what would he know?

"Is she going to be all right for school?" said Caroline.

"What d'you reckon?" said Dad. "Think you ought to stay home?"

Em shook her head. She is one of those strange people who just hates being off school.

"Well, make sure you've got your inhaler. Bitsy, you'll keep an eye on her, won't you?"

So now Dad was asking me too! Of course I promised I would, though really and truly, once we're at school, we don't see that much of each other.

"I think she should stay at home," said Caroline.

"No!" Em shook her head again; quite violently this time. "I want to go!"

"It's not so much a question of what you want," said Caroline, "as of what's good for you."

If she kept on like that she would make Em even more upset. Em can be quite stubborn.

"Bitsy'll watch out for her," said Dad. He made another move to ruffle Em's hair. Em dodged, just in time. "Take it easy, OK?"

By the time we arrived home from school Em was back to normal, but Caroline had obviously been going over things in her mind.

"I can't help feeling," she said, "that it's not very wise to have the cat sleeping with her at night."

Em looked stricken.

I said, "Bella!"

"Sorry?" said Caroline.

"Bella." I pointed at her, curled in a happy heap on Em's lap. "She's Bella!"

"So if Emily's allergic, she really shouldn't have her in her room."

"But Bella always sleeps with Em," I said. "Anyway, Em's allergic to lots of things, not just Bella."

As soon as I'd said it, I knew I'd made a mistake. I should have said Bella was one of the things Em *wasn't* allergic to. Trying my best to stand up for her, like I'd promised Cass, I'd now gone and made things worse!

"Cats are notorious for causing allergies," said Caroline. "Not really the best sort of pet for her to have."

In this very small, faltering voice Em said, "D-dad?" She had started wheezing again. Even Dad noticed. He said, "Don't worry, sweetie, nothing's going to happen to Bella! But I do think Caroline's right about her sleeping in your room. It's asking for trouble."

"In any case," said Caroline, "shouldn't cats be put outside at night?"

"No!" Em clutched at Bella as if Caroline were going to tear her away right there and then. "It's not safe – she'd get run over!"

"Well, all right, if you say so, but at least close your bedroom door so she can't get in. It's not good for you to be so stressed."

Knowing Em, I thought that she would be far more stressed by *not* being allowed to have Bella sleep with her. She tried appealing again to Dad, but Dad was very firmly on Caroline's side.

"Bella shouldn't have been let into your room in the first place," he said. "It's my fault! I should have kept an eye on things." Dad turned to Caroline. "Might be best if we shut her in the kitchen."

"I always thought they went outside," said Caroline.

Not even Dad would agree to Bella being put

outside. He still muttered about the kitchen, but Em gave him such a look, like he was sticking daggers in her heart, that he gave way and agreed she could have the run of the house.

So then she spent half the night yowling piteously on the landing and scraping first at Em's door and then at mine, until in the end I couldn't stand it any longer, the thought of that poor little cat being banished from her nice cosy bed. If she couldn't sleep with Em, she could sleep with me! I went out to get her, only to bump into Em on the same mission.

"Shh!" Em put a finger to her lips. "Don't tell anyone!"

I promised that I wouldn't say a word. Em slipped back into her room with a loudly purring Bella clasped in her arms. Em is normally *such* a law-abiding person. I am the one that breaks the rules and gets into trouble. But we have had Bella since she was a tiny ball of fluff and Em is fiercely protective. I just hoped she didn't wake up in one of her states.

Even if she did, it wouldn't have anything to do with Bella. It would be cos she felt under attack. *Too pale, too thin. Have a sausage roll!* Cass was right, I had to watch out for her.

# CHAPTER EIGHT

Em was happy when she came downstairs next morning. No huffing or puffing or wheezing.

Caroline said, "There! What did I tell you? Shut the cat out and there's no problem."

Em and I exchanged glances. I nearly giggled, but

just managed to stop myself. The last thing we wanted was Caroline asking me what was so funny.

Dad said, "It should have happened a long time ago. And look at her!" He nodded at Bella, sitting on her elbows on top of the fridge. "She obviously wasn't bothered."

Em caught my arm in a vice-like grip. Just as well or I might not have been able to stop myself. Giggles would have come hiccupping out of me and then even Dad would have wondered what was going on.

Em was still happy when she came home from school that afternoon. She even told me that she had found a new friend. Someone called Jenny, whose mum helped run a local animal sanctuary. She said that although she and Jenny were in the same year they'd never really got to know each other before. Now, suddenly, it was like they were best mates. Jenny was going to come round to meet Bella, and Em was going to go round to Jenny's to meet some of the rescued animals. She sounded really excited.

She was still bubbling away when Dad and Caroline arrived home. And then we all sat down to tea and everything changed. Dad and Caroline were having beef lasagne; me and Em were having tomato bake. Playfully, heaping lasagne on to her fork and waving it at us, Caroline said, "Anyone tempted?"

Em shrank back.

"I warn you, I'm not going to give up! Flora? Are you feeling brave?"

I said, "No, cos that's dead cow, and cows *definitely* have faces."

"Bitsy!" Dad leant across and tapped the back of my hand. "Do you mind?"

"Well, they do," I said. I couldn't just sit there and let poor Em be bullied. I had to stick up for her! "And anyway," I said, "you're supposed to be calling me Flora."

"Maybe –" Caroline wafted the fork in my direction

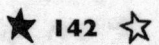 142 ☆

– "maybe you only get to be called a grown-up name like Flora if you start eating grown-up meals like the rest of us."

"You could just try it," pleaded Dad. "One little bite wouldn't hurt you."

I waited for Em to say something, but she had her head bent over her plate. I noticed that she had started wheezing again.

"Go on!" urged Dad. "I dare you! Give it a go."

Em made a sudden choking sound, pushed back her chair and fled from the room.

"Now you've upset her," I said.

"Oh, come on!" said Dad. "I was only joking."

"She does tend to overdramatise," said Caroline. "She's terribly intense, isn't she?"

"She just cares about animals," I said.

"To the point of obsession. It can't be good for her! I feel there's a sort of imbalance, somewhere."

"When we were little," I said, "we found a dead mouse and Em made a tiny coffin for it and buried it in the flower bed. She even made a little headstone. Everybody said how sweet it was."

Dad looked uncomfortable, like, perhaps he should have told her not to be silly.

"And if ever we go out and it's been raining and there's worms all lying about on the pavement, she'll pick them up and put them back on the grass so they can burrow down again."

Caroline shuddered.

"And spiders," I said. "She's always rescuing spiders. Even wasps. If there's a wasp can't find its way out sh—"

"Enough!" Caroline held up her hands. "I'm sure she's very soft-hearted, but this food thing is making her neurotic."

*It wouldn't*, I thought, *if she were just left to herself.*

"The thing is," said Dad, "no one is asking her to become a fully fledged carnivore. We don't expect her to eat raw steaks, or even roast beef, if it comes to that. Just a bit of chicken now and again…"

"Or fish," said Caroline. "Surely she could eat fish?"

I gave her this reproachful look. "Fish have faces," I said.

"Oh!" cried Caroline. "Not that again! Honestly, I give up."

"Don't do that," begged Dad. "She needs someone like you to take her in hand."

I said, "Why?"

There was a silence. I think perhaps I might have sounded a bit aggressive. Caroline raised both her eyebrows, one after the other. Dad looked at me and frowned.

"I don't think that was really necessary," he said, "was it?"

I mumbled that I was sorry. "I just wondered why Em needed to be taken in hand."

"Possibly because neither of you," said Dad, "has had enough discipline in your lives – which is my fault! My fault entirely – and Em is paying the price. I know

★ 145 ☆

she loves animals, I know she cares deeply about them, but she's making herself ill over it. Caroline has her welfare at heart and I think we should back her up."

"We don't want her fading away," said Caroline.

Em has been fading away ever since I can remember. She's always been pale and thin. But here's the thing! Apart from her allergies she's fit as can be. She loves swimming and netball and rounders. She even loves *hockey* – yuck yuck yuck! So I didn't think, really, she was in much danger. If people would just leave her alone!

"Hey!" It was Monday morning. Lottie bounced herself down in the desk next to mine. "I just saw Em. She was wheezing!"

Glumly I said, "I know. It's cos of people having a go at her."

"'bout what?"

"'bout not eating properly."

"Is it Caroline?" Lottie leant eagerly across the gangway. "Is she nagging at her?"

"She doesn't nag, but she's got Dad agreeing with her and it gets Em all upset. I don't think it's right," I said, "people trying to make people eat stuff they don't want to eat."

"They do it all the time," said Lottie. "Like my mum. She's got this thing about sprouts? I mean *sprouts*. Yeeurgh!"

"Sprouts are all right," I said.

"You reckon?" Lottie pulled a face. "Told you your dad would side with Caroline, didn't I? It's what my dad does. Like when I said sprouts made me feel sick he just said, 'Listen to your mum.' Is that what your dad says? 'Listen to Caroline.'?"

"He says we haven't had enough discipline, like Cass didn't look after us properly."

"I'm sure she did her best," said Lottie.

I wasn't sure what that was supposed to mean. It sounded as if it might be some sort of criticism. It was what our PE teacher said, with a big sigh, when I fell off the parallel bars in gym class – "Never mind, Flora. I'm sure you did your best."

"Sounds to me," said Lottie, "like my mum was right. She said Caroline would come as a bit of a rude shock. But then she reckons you must have come as a bit of a rude shock to her as well." Lottie giggled. "I bet she wonders what she's got herself into!"

"Actually, for your information," I said, "she's taking us out for a meal on Friday. It's a celebration, cos it's ten years since she started her employment agency. We're going to this *really expensive* restaurant. *Chateau Bonaparte* or something? Really posh! Dad thought it was just going to be him and her, but Caroline –" I announced it, triumphantly – "Caroline said she wanted us all to go so we could be a proper family. So we can't be *that* much of a rude shock or she wouldn't want to be seen with us!"

Lottie said, "Hmmm," obviously trying to think of some smart remark and not being able to.

"We're going by cab," I said, "so's Dad and Caroline can drink champagne. I expect me and Em will drink some too. Cos of it being a celebration."

"We had champagne at my cousin's wedding," said Lottie. "I didn't like it."

"You probably had cheap stuff," I said.

"It was pink," said Lottie.

I didn't know whether pink was cheap or not.

"Pink is the *best*," said Lottie. "But I still didn't like it."

"Well, anyway," I said, "we're all going to get dressed up cos it's really classy."

"So what are you going to wear?" said Lottie.

"Haven't decided yet. I've got to go through my wardrobe."

"What about Em?"

I squiggled my nose. What *was* Em going to wear? That was a good question. She is seriously useless when it comes to clothes. But as Dad kept anxiously reminding us, "We must make an effort, for Caroline's sake. She wants to feel proud of us!"

He'd even suggested that maybe Em should ask Caroline for advice, which I personally felt was an excellent idea, but when I'd put it to Em a few days ago, she'd giggled in a most un-Em-like way and said it was going to be a surprise.

I reported this to Lottie.

"Uh-oh," said Lottie, rolling her eyes.

I agreed that it was a bit of a worry. I knew for a fact Em hadn't got anything in her wardrobe that could even remotely be called smart.

"Maybe," said Lottie, "we could take her into town after school one day? Help her find something. What d'you think?"

I thought it was a brilliant suggestion. I told Lottie so, and she looked pleased.

"Maybe tomorrow?"

"That," I said, "is what I call a plan!"

But Em was having none of it.

"Honestly," she said, "I've got it all worked out… Jenny's going to help me."

Her new friend Jenny. I just hoped Jenny could be relied on!

Friday evening, soon as I'd finished getting ready, I went to check on Em and see how she was managing.

"Em?" I stuck my head round her door. "Are you— Oh!" I blinked. "Is that what you're going in?"

Em, looking bashful, said, "Do you think it's all right?" .

I said, "Wow!" She was wearing a black sleeveless jacket over a white shirt, with black shorts and long boots that I'd never seen before. Actually, I couldn't remember seeing any of it before. It certainly hadn't come out of her wardrobe.

Anxiously she said, "Is it OK?"

"It's cool," I said. It was! I wouldn't have minded it for myself. "Where d'you get it?"

Two happy spots of colour appeared in Em's cheeks. Now that she had my approval she didn't mind me seeing how excited she was.

 151 ☆

"I went shopping with Jenny! I told her I didn't know what I was going to wear cos I hadn't really got anything, and Dad wanted us to look smart, so we went into town together and Jen helped me choose." Em laughed a bit breathlessly. "I didn't have enough money for a whole new outfit so she's lent me her boots, which is really nice of her cos they're like brand new – she hasn't even worn them, hardly!"

I thought that Jenny must be a really good friend. I was pleased that Em had found someone. She is basically quite a shy sort of person and it isn't always easy for her.

"So what do you think?" She was looking at me eagerly. "Do you really think it's OK?"

I said again that it was cool. "Super cool!"

"But do you really think it suits me?"

I hesitated. And then, seeing Em's face fall and all her new-found confidence suddenly begin to drain away, I said, "I do! I think it's brilliant! Let's go and show Caroline. She won't half be surprised!"

Dad was downstairs, all posh in a suit. He seemed a bit taken aback at the sight of Em in her new trendy gear.

"Have I ever seen that get-up?" he said.

Em giggled. Partly, I think, out of nervousness.

"Don't you think it's cool?" I said.

"It's certainly… unusual," said Dad. He sounded almost as nervous as Em. "Are those –" he waved a hand – "shorts, or what?"

I said, "They're shorts. Why?"

"Just asking," said Dad. "I suppose shorts are all right."

I could see that Em was starting to feel unsure all over again. Rather crossly I said, "Why shouldn't they be?"

Dad hunched a shoulder, like, *Don't ask me, I'm just a man.*

I said, "*Da-a-ad!*" It wasn't like they were *short* shorts. Obviously you couldn't wear *short* shorts. Not to a classy restaurant. But Em's were as long as a skirt would have been. They were perfectly decent! And actually Em has quite nice legs. Nice and slim. Not podgy like mine. I reckoned Dad ought to be pleased to see her all dressed up for once.

"Maybe we should ask Caroline," he said. "Caroline! Come and help us out. Is it all right for Em to wear shorts?"

"Shorts?" Caroline sounded alarmed even before she was properly in the room. She took one look at Em and shrieked, "Emily, my God! You're not going like that?"

A terrible silence fell. Em's cheeks had turned a painful scarlet.

"Sorry," said Caroline. "Sorry! It was just a bit of a shock. But really, sweetie, you can't go to a top-class restaurant dressed like a— Well! In shorts and a leather jacket. It's just not appropriate. Come!" She took Em by the hand. "Let's go back upstairs and see what else you've got. You must have *something*!"

Dad cleared his throat. "That was unfortunate," he said, as Em and Caroline left the room. "She'd obviously made an effort. It just wasn't quite… right. For the occasion."

"I thought she looked lovely," I said.

"Yes, if she was going to a party, maybe. It's not really the sort of thing to wear to a restaurant! We're not just popping up the road for a pizza, you know. This is a place where they won't let you in without a tie."

"Just as well we didn't try going there before," I said. "They'd never have let us in. You didn't even have a tie!"

"Of course I had a tie." Dad was beginning to sound a trifle frazzled. "I had lots of ties. I just never wore them. There's the cab! Go and see if your sister's ready."

Em was on her way back down, pale, now, and subdued, trailing behind Caroline. She had changed into a boring pleated skirt and a thick woolly jumper that our gran had knitted. At least Caroline had let her keep the boots. I was glad about that.

As we walked out to the cab Em whispered urgently in my ear, "The jacket isn't really leather!"

"Makes it even more cool," I said.

# CHAPTER NINE

We'd never been anywhere as posh as the *Chateau Bonaparte*. It was awesome! We were led to our table across oceans of carpet so thick it was like walking on sponge cake. *Triple* sponge cake. You just sank right in up to your ankles.

The table had a white cloth, all stiff and starchy. I

surreptitiously tried folding one of the bits that hung over the edge and it practically cracked in two. The chairs were tiny and spidery, like doll's-house chairs. Dad looked quite precarious, perched on his. I wondered what they would do if a huge great fat person came walking in. Maybe they had special chairs they kept in a cupboard. Or maybe they had rules about fat people. At least I could see now why Caroline had made Em go and change her clothes. A sleeveless jacket and shorts would have been a bit out of place. They might not even have let her in.

"Right," said Caroline. She reached out for the menu. "Let's take a look and see what you two fussypants can eat."

The menu was all in French. *And* in handwriting. Dad chuckled.

"This will test you," he said.

Em and I peered at it distrustfully.

"*Potage*," I said. "That's soup!"

Em said, "Yes, and *boeuf* is beef."

"And *oignon* is onion," said Dad. "French onion soup! Can't get more veggie than that."

"Or more tasty," said Caroline.

Rather doubtfully, we agreed to try the onion soup. It seemed to be the only veggie starter on offer so we didn't really have much choice.

"Good," said Dad. "That's that settled. How about the main course?"

There was only one veggie dish and that was aubergine. Em and I exchanged worried glances. We don't like aubergine!

"Don't like aubergine?" Caroline tutted impatiently. "How awkward you are!"

I didn't think we were awkward. I thought it was the restaurant that was awkward. Seemed to me it wasn't fair, only having one dish for vegetarians and a whole load for meat-eaters. I counted them up — there were *ten*. I didn't say anything, though. It would have been rude to grumble when Caroline was treating us.

"So what are we going to do?" she said. She studied the menu. "How about roast potatoes and a selection of vegetables? Would that suit you?"

We nodded. By now I was starting to feel a bit uncertain, what with the menu being all in French and the waiter standing there looking superior, like we were some low form of life that had crawled out of the gutter. Caroline had explained that we not only didn't eat meat, we didn't eat fish, either, and he'd made a puffing sound like *pfui!* Like, really snooty. I'd been tempted to open my mouth and say about fish having faces, but a warning glare from Caroline had stopped me.

"Well, now," said Dad, when we'd all settled on what we were having, "isn't this nice?" He beamed happily. "All together, as a family! You can thank Caroline for that. If it had been up to me I'd have left you both at home to eat lettuce leaves. So let's not make any waves, huh?"

"Have a roll and butter," said Caroline. "You can't object to that."

"They're not going to object to anything," said Dad. "Are you?"

Very meekly we shook our heads.

"Shall we let them have a taste of champagne?" said Dad. "Do you think they deserve it?"

"Oh, I think so," said Caroline. "They've behaved quite well so far."

I felt Em kick at me under the table. She pulled a face. I pulled one back. I wondered, if Em hadn't been there, whether I would have been tempted to eat prawns. People at the next table were eating them and just for a moment I almost forgot that even little creatures like prawns have faces. Sort of. But I had to support Em. Apart from anything else, I'd promised Cass.

The champagne arrived in a big silver bucket full of ice.

"Oh," I said, "I thought it would be pink."

"Why so?" said Dad.

"Cos pink's the best!"

"Who told you that?" Caroline sounded amused.

"*Isn't* it?" I said.

"Not really. You just pay over the odds for the pretty colour."

Huh! I might have known Lottie had no idea what she was talking about.

"They use exactly the same grapes," Dad assured me. "They just add the skins to make it pink."

I felt my eyes widen. "Champagne's made from *grapes*?"

Caroline laughed. "What did you think it was made from?"

"Dunno," I said. I'd never thought about it. But just to get things straight, I said, "So pink isn't any better than the ordinary sort? Like that one?" I waved a hand at the bottle of champagne sitting in its ice bucket.

"This is vintage," said Dad.

"Is vintage good?"

"You'd better believe it! The amount it costs."

"So is vintage the best?"

"What is this *obsession*?" said Caroline.

"I'm just trying to learn," I said. "What make is it? The one we're having?" I needed to know so that I could tell Lottie.

"This is Bollinger," said Dad.

"*Bollinger?*" I giggled.

"Strange, whimsical child," said Caroline. "What do you find so funny?"

"Sounds rude," I said.

Caroline rolled her eyes.

"So, are you going to try it?" said Dad.

"Yes, please!"

I held out my glass. The waiter, with a sneery sort of smirk, splashed a bit of champagne into it. I felt like hissing *Bollinger!* at him. He was being really obnoxious.

"There you go," said Dad. "Just a taste."

I really wanted to like champagne, just so I could boast about it to Lottie, but quite honestly the only good thing I could find to say about it was the way the bubbles all fizzed and popped. Basically it was like drinking medicine.

Dad said, "Well, that was a waste! You'd better have something else."

"Fruit juice," said Caroline. I'd actually have preferred Coke, but I thought probably they wouldn't do Coke in such a posh restaurant, so I chose pineapple juice to take the taste away, pineapple juice being really sweet. I like sweet things!

I didn't like the onion soup *at all*, even if it was French. I don't think Em did, either, from the way her lips kept puckering. It tasted like a bad smell, like armpits. But we both cleared our soup bowls. We didn't want Dad accusing us of being ungrateful.

He and Caroline were eating lobster for their main course. I could see Em trying not to watch as they tucked into it. We just had our roast potatoes and vegetables.

After a few minutes Dad frowned and said, "Emily, what's the problem?"

"N-nothing," said Em.

"So why do you keep sucking your cheeks in like that?"

Em looked down at her roast potatoes. "They taste funny," she muttered.

"Oh, for heaven's sake!" Dad was starting to sound a bit irritable. "They're only *potatoes*. Bitsy's eating them all right. Aren't you?"

He gave me this look, like, *Don't you dare say otherwise!*

"What's the matter with them?" said Caroline.

Em said that nothing was the matter, they just didn't taste like normal potatoes.

I'd thought the same thing, but decided they were probably just a special brand. Special French potatoes. I said this to Em, and she latched on to it gratefully.

"That's probably what it is."

Frowning, Caroline picked up the menu and studied it for a moment.

"Can't you just enjoy them?" said Dad.

"I am," said Em, hastily stuffing potato into her mouth.

"They're good," I said. "Just different."

"But can you eat them?"

We assured him that we could.

"Thank the lord for that," said Dad.

For afters Caroline said we could choose whatever we fancied. Even lemon possets if they were on the menu. (They weren't. But I bet they wouldn't have been as good as mine, anyway!)

"There's a thing called lemon sorbet," said Em.

I didn't think lemon sorbet sounded very interesting so I had a big gooey meringue thing all squidging with cream. Caroline didn't say a word!

"That was yummy," I said. "Best part of the meal! But I did enjoy the potatoes," I added.

"Oh, me too," said Em.

"Did you really? Honestly?" said Caroline. We promised her that we did. We wanted her to be happy. She gave a little smile. "That's good," she said. "That's excellent!"

It wasn't till we got home and Dad was putting the car away that she told us the truth.

"Girls, I have a confession to make! I didn't say anything at the time because I knew if I did there'd be a scene, but I suddenly realised those potatoes that you liked so much were actually cooked in goose fat. It just never occurred to me until I looked at the menu again. Still..." She gave a little laugh. "No harm done! You managed to eat them quite happily, and it hasn't poisoned you, has it?"

I darted an anxious glance at Em. She had this look of frozen horror on her face. She whispered, "*Goose* fat?"

"I'm sorry," said Caroline, "I wasn't trying to trick you, but the French do pride themselves on their cuisine. There probably wasn't anything on the menu that would qualify as totally vegetarian, apart from the aubergines, which you said you didn't like. And the puddings! You were safe there. You enjoyed those, didn't you?"

She smiled at us hopefully. I darted a quick glance at Em.

Caroline said, "Emily? Am I forgiven?"

Em made a choking sound.

"Oh, now, come on!" said Caroline. "Don't go all to pieces on us. It's not the end of the world."

"It was for the goose," I said.

"The goose was already dead! They don't kill them just to cook potatoes. Emily, do have a sense of proportion!"

But Em had fled the room, bumping into Dad on his way in.

"Now what's up?" said Dad. "Where's she off to in such a rush?"

Caroline shook her head, like, *I give up!*

"She's probably gone to be sick," I said.

"Sick?" Dad sounded alarmed. "Why?"

"We ate goose fat," I said.

"*Goose* fat?"

"On the potatoes!"

"But you enjoyed them," said Caroline.

"Only cos we didn't realise." And anyway, we hadn't enjoyed them. We'd known there was something peculiar about them. *And* the onion soup had tasted like armpits.

"Well, but if you didn't realise…" Dad looked at me, almost pleading. He wanted me to say it was all right. That Em was just making a fuss about nothing.

"Honestly," said Caroline, "I didn't mean to trick them!"

"Of course you didn't." Dad put an arm round her, all protective. "You know these girls… couple of tragedy queens!"

"It's my own fault," said Caroline. "You told me to leave them at home. I just so wanted us to be a family!"

"I know," said Dad. "I know." He patted her shoulder. "I'm afraid you can't take them anywhere!"

I thought that was totally unfair of Dad. Caroline *had* tricked us; I didn't care what she said. Soon as she'd discovered about the potatoes she should have told us, so we could have ordered something else. She didn't have to let us go on eating them. That was just, like, *gross*.

"Do you want to go and check on your sister?" said Dad.

"I'll go, if you like," offered Caroline, "since I'm the one she's cross with."

"She has no right to be cross," said Dad, sounding rather cross himself. "It couldn't be helped, it was a genuine mistake."

"It's all right," I said. "I'll go."

I found Em in the kitchen, sitting at the table cuddling Bella.

"You OK?" I said.

Em nodded.

"Have you been sick?"

"I couldn't help it." Em gazed up at me pathetically. "I've eaten animals!"

"You weren't to know," I said. "Somebody should have told us."

"But what could we have had? There wasn't anything!"

"Apart from aubergines." All slippy and slimy. "And puddings." I brightened. "The puddings were nice!"

"Probably cooked those with something horrible, like gelatine."

"Oh." I'd forgotten about gelatine. I never used to know what it was until Em explained to me. She said we had to watch out for it cos it came from hooves and bones and even *intestines*. Yuck! Doubtfully I said, "They wouldn't use it in meringues, would they?"

"Could have," said Em.

"I don't think so," I said. "Meringues are just egg white and sugar."

"Yes, and you can bet the eggs came from battery hens!"

I said, "Don't! That's horrible."

"It's all horrible." Em snuffled and wiped her nose

on the back of her hand. "I wish Caroline had never taken us!"

"Me too," I said.

"We've just gone and ruined everything."

I said, "*Us?*" What had we done?

"It was meant to be a celebration! It was meant to be *happy*. She just wanted us to enjoy ourselves and now she's all upset and so's Dad."

"So are you," I said. "You're wheezing again."

"Don't tell Caroline," begged Em. "She'll say it's Bella!"

Yes, and Dad would agree with her. That was the worst part of it – Dad always taking Caroline's side.

"It's cos you're stressed," I said. Loyally I added, "Anyone'd be stressed eating goose fat when they're supposed to be vegetarian."

"You're not," said Em.

"I am so! I just don't show it as much."

I wouldn't ever kill an animal for food, not unless I was starving, maybe, but what can you do when someone you trust says "Eat the roast potatoes," knowing all the time they're covered in goose fat? It must have said on the menu, but the menu was all in French. I'd only been learning French for a term!

Dad spoke French. Had *he* read the menu? If he had, then that would be, like, a real betrayal.

"What are you frowning about?" said Em.

"Nothing." I didn't want to upset her even more. It was bad enough Dad thought we were tragedy queens. "Thing is," I said, "we didn't know!"

"It's still murder," said Em. She pushed her hair back and took a quivering breath. "Meat is murder. You know that!"

Em has these posters in her bedroom that tell you so in big red letters like dripping blood. When Caroline first came to live with us she tried to get Em to take them down. She said they were grotesque.

"Why can't you have pictures of pop stars or something?"

She'd even complained to Dad, but for once Dad had stuck up for Em.

"Animal rights are like her religion," he'd said.

The posters had stayed where they were. Caroline said she shuddered every time she had to go into Em's room.

She appeared at the kitchen door just as we were deciding we might as well go to bed.

"Oh, Emily, look at you!" she said. "Look at the state you're in! I hope you're not taking that cat upstairs with you?"

"*I'm* taking her," I said. I snatched Bella away from Em and cradled her defiantly. "She sleeps with me now."

"She shouldn't be sleeping with either of you. What's wrong with out here?"

"She's not used to it," I said.

As soon as we were upstairs I bundled Bella back into Em's waiting arms.

"Don't worry," I said. "She's never going to find out."

I was just drifting off to sleep when there was a tap at the door and Em crept in. She hovered uncertainly.

"Bitsy?" she whispered. "Are you awake?"

"Mm," I grunted into my pillow. "Wosser madder?"

"I just wanted to ask you something. If anything ever happened to me, you would look after Bella, wouldn't you?"

I half sat up, propping myself on an elbow. "What are you talking about?"

"If I wasn't here... I need to make sure she'd be all right."

I said, "Of course she'd be all right! But why wouldn't you be here?"

"Well, like, suppose I got run over or something? These things happen," said Em.

"Not if you remember to look both ways," I said.

Perhaps I shouldn't have said it, but it doesn't do to encourage Em too much when she gets one of her gloomy fits.

"Anyway, thank you for disturbing me," I said. "I'll probably be awake half the night now."

"Sorry," said Em, sounding very crestfallen.

I saw her flit across the room, but even before she was halfway through the door I'd gone back to sleep.

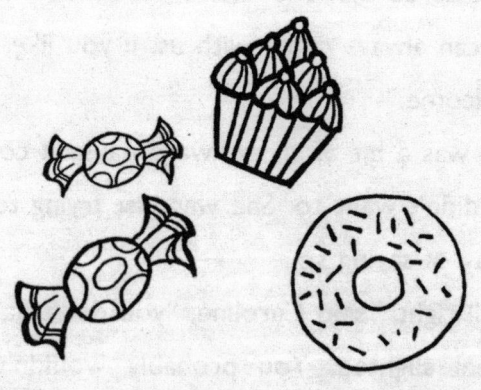

# CHAPTER TEN

Next day was Saturday and Caroline said that she and Dad were going shopping.

"What about you two? What are you two up to?"

I pulled a face and said, "Homework."

"Can't argue with that," said Caroline. "How about you, Emily?"

Em muttered that she hadn't decided.

"You can always come with us, if you like. You're quite welcome."

There was a bit of an awkward pause. I could see that Em didn't want to. She was just trying to find a polite way of saying so.

"It's all right," said Caroline, "you don't have to! I won't feel slighted. You probably wouldn't enjoy it, anyway. We're going to prowl round the antique shops. Aren't we." She turned fondly to Dad.

"This is what I've been told," said Dad. "And as you know, I always do what I'm told!"

Caroline laughed. "You see?" she said. "I've got your dad well trained!"

Dad and Caroline went off, leaving me and Em on our own.

"Are you really going to do homework?" said Em. "On a *Saturday*?"

I said, "Yes. Why?"

"Wouldn't you rather go round and see Lottie?"

"Well, I would," I said, cos who wants to do homework? "But she's not here – they've gone away for the weekend. Plus I've got *mountains* of stuff to get through."

"In that case," said Em, "you'd better go and shut yourself in your room and not come out till you've finished."

"There's no need to get all bossy about it," I said.

"I know what you're like," said Em. "Attention span of a flea."

"So what are you going to do?"

"Just things," said Em.

"What sort of things?"

"*Things.*"

"Well, pardon me for asking," I said.

Always so *secretive.*

I went up to my room, emptied my school bag on the bed and put my headphones on. Then I turned up the volume really LOUD. I find I can work far better if I have a bit of noise going on. It helps me concentrate.

I was concentrating so hard I didn't even notice when Dad and Caroline came back from their shopping trip. Caroline had to come upstairs and find me. She said, "Honestly, Flora, how can you possibly work with that racket going on? I swear I can hear it halfway along the landing! You'll blow your eardrums out."

Proudly I said, "I've done *all* my homework."

"Well, good, I'm glad. But you won't be so happy when you get to be my age and your hearing's gone! Go and tell Emily that lunch is ready, will you?"

"Okey dokey!"

I waltzed along to Em's room and banged on the door.

*"Em! Caroline says lunch is ready."*

"So where is she?" said Caroline, as I went downstairs.

"Dunno," I said.

Caroline tutted impatiently. She had a real thing about us all sitting down at the same time. *And* about people doing what she told them.

"You'd better go and give her another call," she said.

I walked to the foot of the stairs and bellowed, "EM! LUNCH IS READY!" I waited. Anyone bawled as loud as that and *something* would have filtered through, even with headphones on. And Em didn't even have any headphones.

"Where is she?" Caroline had appeared at my side. "What is she doing? *Emily!* Time for lunch."

Still nothing.

"Oh, for goodness' sake!" Caroline set off up the stairs. "Let me go and see what she's up to."

Seconds later, Caroline came back down. "Well, that explains it. She's not there!"

"Not there?" Dad had come into the hall to see what all the fuss was about.

"No," said Caroline. "Emily's not there and that cat is on her bed."

"So where's Emily?"

They both turned to look at me.

"Where's she gone?" said Dad.

"Didn't know she'd gone anywhere," I said. "I thought she was in her room."

Caroline's forehead knitted itself into an irritated frown. "You mean she's gone waltzing off somewhere and didn't bother telling you?"

"That's not at all like Emily," said Dad.

"Oh, come on! She's a teenager. Totally thoughtless."

"Bitsy might be," said Dad. "Not Em."

I resented that. I said, "Excuse me, but I think all the time!"

"I'm sure you do," said Caroline. "Let's sit down and eat. Emily will just have to fend for herself."

By the time we'd finished lunch it was two o'clock and still no sign of Em.

"Bitsy, didn't you even hear her go out?" said Dad.

"Flora wouldn't have heard if a bomb had gone off." Caroline clattered plates and dishes on to a tray. "She has that music up so loud it's a wonder she hasn't deafened herself."

"I was doing my homework," I said. "I was *concentrating*."

"I take it you've tried her mobile?"

"Can't," I said.

"Why not?"

"She put it in the washing machine."

"She did *what?*"

"It was a mistake," I said.

"So I would imagine!"

"It was in the back pocket of her jeans; she forgot it was there. It got all waterlogged. She kept hoping if she dried it out it'd start working again. Which it sort of did," I added, "but then it went funny. I've got one," I added, trying to be helpful. "She sometimes uses mine."

"So would she have taken it with her, do you think?"

I said no, mine was upstairs in my bedroom.

Caroline made an impatient clicking noise with her tongue. "This really is very naughty of her."

"Are you quite sure," said Dad, "she didn't mention

anything about going off to… I don't know! See a friend? Who was that friend she used to have? Jane, or Janet, or someone?"

I said, "Janis. She went to Australia. Ages ago."

"Oh. Well! Who is she friends with now? There must be someone!"

"Jenny," I said. "She's friends with Jenny."

"So do we have Jenny's number anywhere?"

"Dunno."

"Oh, Flora, for heaven's sake!" Caroline was starting to sound like she'd had enough of me and Em. "Try to make a bit of an effort, can't you?"

Aggrieved, I said, "Well, but I don't know! They only got to be friends quite recently. I don't know anything about her." And then I suddenly remembered. "Oh, yes, I do! Her mum runs an animal sanctuary or something."

"Well, that's a start," said Dad. "Let's see what happens if we put it into Google."

I said, "Put what in?"

"Animal sanctuaries, Brighton… There we are! Loads of them. Pigeons? Horses?"

"Dogs," I said. "I think."

"OK… still quite a few. What's Jenny's surname?"

"Dun—" I stopped. "I don't know."

"What about this one?" Dad pointed at the screen. "Paws Animal Sanctuary. Small-animal rescue. They're local. Let's give them a go."

"You do that," said Caroline. "We'll get on with the washing-up."

I'd rather have stayed and listened to Dad on the telephone, but I'd already learnt that when Caroline wanted something done, it was best to do it straight away.

"Has Emily always been a problem?" she said. "She seems very troubled."

"She's sensitive," I said.

"Well, I suppose that's one way of putting it. Spoilt might be another way."

"Em's not spoilt!" I said.

"You think? I'd say that's exactly what she was! All I ever hear is 'Poor Emily, we have to make allowances for her, we—' Ah, Donald!" She broke off as Dad appeared. "Any luck?"

"Not really," said Dad. "It was the right place, but her mum said Jenny was out riding and as far as she was aware she hadn't seen Emily since they left school yesterday."

"So that was a dead end." Caroline thrust a tea towel at me. "Don't just stand around, Flora. Things can't come to a full stop simply because your sister chooses to go flouncing off without telling anyone."

Slowly and resentfully I picked up a bunch of cutlery. Seemed to me that finding Em was a whole lot more important than wiping up a load of wet knives and forks.

"You don't think she could have gone to see Cass and Becky?" I said.

"Without telling anyone?" Caroline's eyebrows flew back into her hairline. "Without asking permission?"

"She might have done."

Dad brightened. "I'll give them a call! I guess they'll be at the shop."

"Not on a Saturday," I said.

"What?" Dad's thumb was already hovering over the keypad.

"She and Becky don't work Saturdays any more."

"Don't work Saturdays?" Caroline's eyebrows, which had just come down, promptly shot back up again. Up down, up down, like yo-yos. "What kind of shop doesn't open on a Saturday?"

"They're open," I said. "They just don't go in. They have special Saturday people."

"Since when?" said Dad.

"Since Cass went to live with Becky."

"Well, I never." Dad scratched his head. "Why doesn't anyone ever tell me anything?"

"They probably did," said Caroline. She said it quite tartly, like Dad being so absent-minded didn't amuse her any more. "Try them at home."

Obediently, Dad did so. He shook his head. "It's on answerphone."

"So try her mobile!"

But Cass's mobile was on answerphone too.

"Now what?" said Dad.

He was starting to look quite worried. Even I was a bit concerned. It was *so* not like Em to just go off without telling anyone.

I had a sudden idea. "How about Polly? Maybe she's gone to see Polly!"

"Who's Polly?" said Caroline.

"She works with Dad. She's in his department."

"Oh, I remember! Looks like she lives on muesli."

What did that mean? What was wrong with muesli? Cass had sometimes given it to us for breakfast.

"Polly," said Dad, "happens to have an extremely fine brain." He said it, for Dad, quite sharply. Caroline pulled a face. "I don't quite get, though, why Em should suddenly want to go and see her?"

"We *like* Polly," I said. "She's our *friend*."

"True," said Dad. To Caroline he explained, "They've always been very close to Polly. They've known her a long time. Let me go and get her number."

"Is it too much to ask," wondered Caroline, as Dad left the room, "why he doesn't have it on his mobile phone?"

Apologetically I said, "I don't think he knows how to do it."

"No? Well, that figures. I guess they didn't have mobiles in the eighteenth century."

I couldn't understand why all of a sudden Caroline was being so mean. Acting like she thought Dad was an idiot. I bet he knows more about the eighteenth century than almost anyone else alive!

"Flora, are you *absolutely certain*," said Caroline, "you really have *no idea* where your sister's gone?"

She was giving me this suspicious glare, like Mr Hendricks at school when he thinks you're not telling the truth about why you haven't done your maths homework. Usually, with maths homework, he's right. But I really *didn't* know where Em had gone.

"Well." Dad was back. Just in time to save me from the third degree. "She's not with Polly, though apparently she did speak to her on the phone the other day. Did you know that?"

I shook my head.

"Neither did I," said Dad. "It seems she asked Polly not to say anything."

"Why would she do that?" said Caroline.

"According to Polly, she didn't want me to be worried."

"About what?"

"Oh…" Dad waved a hand. "Bits and pieces that have been troubling her. I don't know!"

"If you ask me," said Caroline, "that girl is far too intense. I sometimes seriously wonder whether she should see a therapist."

For the first time ever – well, the first time since Caroline had come to live with us – I saw a faint shadow of annoyance cross Dad's face.

"There's nothing wrong with Em," he said. "She just feels things a bit more deeply than the rest of us. Bitsy, can I have a word with you? In the other room?"

"Just let me know when you're through," said Caroline. She reached across and whisked the tea towel away from me. "I wouldn't want to intrude!"

# CHAPTER ELEVEN

"Right. Now!" Dad sat down beside me on the sofa. "What's going on with your sister? Why did she feel the need to ring Polly?"

"We like Polly," I said. "We like her a *lot.*"

"Yes, I hear you! But why did Em ring her?"

"I don't know! She didn't tell me."

"You don't think she's still upset over last night? About those wretched potatoes? Because if she is, she's not being fair! Caroline honestly didn't mean to trick her."

"It's not just that," I muttered.

"So what is it? Say something!"

I picked up Bella, who had come wobbling in, and buried my face in her neck.

"Look," said Dad, "we're by ourselves. Whatever it is, you can tell me."

I stayed silent, rubbing my cheek against Bella's fur.

"Bitsy, this is serious," said Dad. "Speak to me! Em wasn't hurt, was she, because of Caroline asking her to change her clothes? I mean, even I could see that shorts weren't the right thing to wear."

"She chose that outfit *specially*," I said, "cos she wanted to look nice."

"And she did look nice! Very nice. It just wasn't... appropriate."

"She didn't know! How was she to know? She's not into fashion."

"She could have asked Caroline."

"Caroline said she looked frumpy."

"When?" Dad sounded like he found that difficult to believe. "When did Caroline say she looked frumpy?"

"Ages ago. When she started on about her eating meat."

"Oh," said Dad. "So that's what it's about. Caroline's genuinely concerned for her, you know."

"Like telling her she can't sleep with Bella!" I squeezed Bella as I said it. She gave a little protesting squeak.

Gravely Dad said, "I tend to be with her on that one."

"But she's always slept with Bella! It's only since Caroline came she's started getting stressed."

"Stressed?" Dad looked stricken. "*Em?* What are you saying? I thought you were all getting on so well!"

"We were," I said. "But then you keep taking Caroline's side all the time and it's always Em that makes excuses and—"

"Whoa! Slow down," said Dad. "What do you mean, *Em makes excuses*? Excuses for what? For me?"

"For Caroline! Like when Caroline says things that upset her, Em says it's not her fault, she's just trying to help."

"Well, but she is," said Dad. "She's trying her best to be a good stepmum!"

I didn't say anything to that, just kept my head in Bella's fur.

"You don't think she is?" said Dad.

I shrugged. "Dunno. Maybe."

"All right," Dad sighed. "What sort of thing does she say that upsets Em so much?"

"Well, like Em ought to eat meat cos it might help her hair, or—"

"Help her *hair*? What's wrong with her hair?"

"You wouldn't know," I said, "cos you're a man and

you don't ever notice, but Em's really sensitive about it. She reckons it's too thin."

"So obviously Caroline was concerned for her."

I said, "Yes, but she picks on her. She makes her feel bad about herself. And Em tried so hard," I said. "She so wants you to be happy!"

There was a bit of a pause after I said this. I glanced up at Dad. He was looking quite shaken.

"Em wants me to be happy?" he said.

"Yes! We both do. We promised Cass. Cos we think you deserve it!"

"Now you're starting to make me feel guilty." Dad ran his fingers through his hair, sticking it all up on end like a porcupine. "I had no idea! I should have spoken to her. Last night. I should have had a word with her. If anything's—" He broke off. "Bitsy? What are you thinking?"

"I've just remembered…" My voice came out in a whisper. "Last night… she made me promise to… to look after Bella if…"

"If what?"

"If anything happened to her!"

"Oh, my God." I could see the colour draining out of Dad's face. "What time was this?"

"Just after we'd gone to bed."

"Did she seem… distressed?"

I crinkled my nose. "She was upset cos she thought she'd gone and ruined the evening for you."

"Oh, Bitsy! As if that mattered."

"She really really w—"

My voice froze abruptly as the telephone rang.

"I'll get it!"

Dad went racing out to the hall, almost bumping into Caroline on the way. Caroline stood hovering in the doorway. I strained forward on the sofa, my heart hammering. Dad said, "Cass?" And then he leant across and pulled the door shut, forcing Caroline back into the living room. We just heard him say, "Thank God for that!"

Caroline looked across at me and pulled a face.

"Obviously found her. I guess she went to lick her wounds and get a bit of sympathy."

I couldn't think what to say. We sat in silence, waiting for Dad to come back. If Caroline hadn't been there I'd have gone and listened at the door. I couldn't think why Dad had closed it. Didn't he want us to hear? Or didn't he want *Caroline* to hear? I felt there was something going on between him and Caroline, like when me and Lottie fall out with each other there's all this prickly kind of tension. But Dad and Caroline hadn't fallen out! Not as far as I knew.

"I take it you've managed to locate her?" said Caroline as Dad reappeared.

"Is she all right?" I leant forward, accidentally squeezing Bella, who gave a protesting yowl. "Dad? Is she OK?"

"Relax," said Dad. "She's fine."

Caroline made a snorting sound, like, "Hmph!"

"Why didn't Cass answer her phone?"

"Apparently she switched it off yesterday evening when she and Becky went to a show."

"And didn't think to switch it on again," Caroline nodded. "That figures."

A slight frown rumpled Dad's brow.

"So why on earth," said Caroline, "didn't she call you the minute Emily turned up?"

"She and Becky have been out all morning. They found her waiting for them when they got back. The poor girl had been sitting on the doorstep for hours."

"And of course *she* wouldn't have thought to call and let you know where she was? Just sat there, while we all chewed our nails imagining the worst."

"She is going to come back?" I said.

"Cass is keeping her overnight. I said we'd go down in the morning and fetch her."

"Honestly!" Caroline made one of her impatient scoffing noises. "There is simply no excuse for this sort of behaviour! Talk about selfish."

Dad said, "Being unhappy can make you selfish."

Caroline turned sharply. "What on earth does she have to be unhappy about?"

"You made her eat goose fat!" I cried.

"Oh, Flora, for goodness' sake! I didn't *make* her, it was a genuine mistake. In any case, it's hardly any reason to go flouncing off like some spoilt little madam, causing us all this grief and heartache."

I didn't honestly think that Caroline had been caused any grief or heartache. Only me and Dad.

"Frankly," said Dad, "I'm just thankful to know that she's safe."

"You shouldn't have to be thankful. It's ridiculous! All this fuss over a little bit of goose fat, scarcely enough to taste."

"I could taste it," I said.

"Yes, well, you would, wouldn't you," said Caroline.

"You *tricked* us," I said.

Two angry spots of colour came splashing on to Caroline's cheeks. "I was just trying to give us a good evening. I thought we might manage to enjoy ourselves for once, without all this hysterical nonsense from Emily."

I opened my mouth to protest. *Someone* had to stick up for Em. But Dad had taken me by the shoulders and was gently but very firmly propelling me towards the door.

"Not now, Bitsy."

"But, Dad," I said, "I—"

*"Not now, Bitsy!"*

"But I—"

"Bitsy, please," said Dad. "This is between me and Caroline."

I suppose, really, I should have gone up to my room or into the kitchen. Anywhere I couldn't be tempted to eavesdrop. But how could I help it? This was about Em! I had to know what was going on.

I crouched at the foot of the stairs, ready to spring up and make a dash for it the minute the door opened. I wished I'd brought Bella with me.

There is something very comforting about cuddling a cat.

I heard Dad's voice, like a sort of low rumble. Then Caroline's, lighter and sharper. Just at first I couldn't make out what they were saying. They seemed to be having some sort of disagreement. Was it about Em? Was it about me?

I leant forward, straining to hear. Caroline's voice rose angrily.

"This is absolutely classic! Evil stepmum can't do anything right!"

Dad's voice rumbled something in reply.

"If she feels like that," snapped Caroline, "it might be better if she *did* go and live with Cass!"

And now Dad's voice was raised as well. "I'm not having one of my daughters turned out of her own house!"

"Maybe I should be turned out? Is that what you're saying?"

I couldn't hear whether it was or not cos Dad's

voice had gone back to its rumbling. He rumbled for some time and when Caroline started speaking again it was very quiet and intense so that now I couldn't hear either of them.

I went on crouching for a bit longer, but it didn't seem like they were going to start up again. In the end shame overcame me, or maybe it was just that I couldn't hear anything any more, so I uncrouched myself and went up to my room. I sat for a while on the bed, toying with my phone, wondering whether to ring Cass. There wasn't any reason I shouldn't. I could ring Cass if I wanted!

And then I thought that maybe it would be like betraying Dad, cos I knew if I started talking to Cass it would all come tumbling out, the way words do, like something's burst and you just can't stop. Before I knew it I'd be telling her about Dad and Caroline and the things they'd said to each other. But I had to ring someone!

I could ring Lottie. She was at her gran's, but Lottie's always eager to chat.

"Lots?" I said. "That you?"

"Dunno," said Lottie. "Might be. Depends who's calling."

"You know who's calling!"

Lottie giggled. "Might do. Might not."

"Stop messing around," I said. "I've got stuff to tell you!"

"Ooh, what?" said Lottie. She loves a bit of gossip. Well, who doesn't? "Tell, tell!"

"I can't actually say at the moment," I said.

"Why not?"

"Cos I can't. I'll tell you Monday."

"Oh, please," begged Lottie. "Tell me now, Bitsy! *Please?*"

"Can't," I said. "My lips are sealed."

"So why bother ringing me?"

"Thought you'd like something to look forward to."

"You mean you thought it'd be fun to just wind me up!"

"Well, that too," I said.

"*Grunge* bucket!" yelled Lottie.

We rang off, very happy with each other. It's one of our things, calling each other rude names. Back in Year Six, I used to call Lottie *Mistress Mildew*. I wasn't quite sure what it meant, but it seemed like a good name for her. She used to call me Pudding Face. Now I was Grunge Bucket. At least I preferred it to Pudding Face.

I felt a whole lot better after my exchange with Lottie. It was like a bit of normality in the midst of all the upset.

I went back downstairs quite cheerfully, almost managing to forget that Em had run away and that Dad and Caroline had had a fight. I could tell, though, from the atmosphere that they hadn't made up. Caroline was all tight-lipped and Dad was even more bumbling than usual. It wasn't at all a comfortable kind of evening. I went to bed, without even having to be told, at nine o'clock. Generally Caroline and I had a bit of a battle about it, but it

was like she wasn't talking to me any more and
Dad was reading students' essays, so I just took
myself off.

Not even sure anyone noticed.

# CHAPTER TWELVE

Next morning, me and Dad drove to Lewes to pick up Em. Caroline stayed behind. She and Dad weren't really talking, so I guessed they must still be cross with each other. Dad didn't talk to me very much, either, on the way down. I kept trying to make conversation, like "What a beautiful day it is," and "Oh, Dad, look at that lovely graveyard," cos normally he encourages us to comment on things, and I mean, you can't just sit in total silence mile after mile.

But no matter how hard I tried, Dad didn't respond. Sometimes he grunted; at other times he didn't even seem to realise that I'd said anything. I just hoped he was keeping his eyes on the road, cos Dad is *so* not a good driver.

"*Da-a-ad!*" I screamed at him, as we whizzed past our turning. "We should have gone left!"

Dad heaved a sigh. "Sorry. Preoccupied. Can I turn round?"

"Dad, *no*," I said.

We had to drive on another couple of miles to the next roundabout. Caroline would not have found it amusing. She seemed to have lost all patience with Dad's absent-mindedness.

Em and Cass were waiting for us at the front door. Em stood uncertainly.

"Sweetheart, it's all right," said Dad. He held out his arms and with a stifled sob Em ran into them.

"Where's Becky?" I said.

"She's gone to open up the shop. Come inside."

We followed Cass indoors.

"You two girls wait there," said Dad. "I just need a quick word with your aunt."

Em and I perched awkwardly on a couple of stools in the kitchen.

"Dad and Caroline had a row," I said.

Em immediately looked apprehensive. "About what?"

I almost said "About you!", but just in time I managed to bite the words back. I do *occasionally* stop to think before I speak.

"Dunno," I said. "But they're not talking."

"Is that why she didn't come with you?"

"I guess."

Em bit her lip.

"We'd have got here sooner," I said, "if Caroline

had been driving. Know that bit at the bottom of the hill where we have to make a left? Dad went and missed it! So then he wanted to do a *U*-turn! I had to stop him. You're not allowed to do U-turns," I said. "Not on that road. You'd think he'd have learnt by now."

"He needs a satnav," said Em.

"Knowing Dad, he'd probably end up at John o'Groats."

"Don't be cross with him," begged Em. "He can't help it!"

It wasn't what Caroline would have said. Caroline would have said he was a grown man and ought to start being a bit more responsible. She'd been saying a lot of things like that just recently.

"Hey, I looked after Bella for you," I said.

"Thank you," said Em humbly.

"I let her sleep on my bed. Don't think she likes it as much as yours, though. She'll be ever so pleased to see you!"

Em gave a faint, watery smile, after which we both lapsed into silence.

We still didn't really talk much on the way home. Em sat in front with Dad, keeping an eye on the road, while I sat in the back and racked my brains for things to say and couldn't think of any.

On the outskirts of Brighton, Dad suggested we stop somewhere for Sunday lunch.

"That would be fun," he said, "wouldn't it?"

I agreed that it would. It was Em who said, "What about Caroline?"

"Don't worry about Caroline," said Dad.

"But she likes us all to sit down as a family!"

"She won't mind. Let's go and look for one of those veggie places Cass is always banging on about."

When we arrived home we found Bella asleep on the kitchen table. Em swooped on her immediately. As she did so, an envelope went skating to the ground.

"Ooh, what's that?" I snatched at it. "Dad, it's for you!"

Dad said, "Yes. It'll be from Caroline."

"Aren't you going to read it?"

"I can guess what it says. But all right, if you want me to."

Dad opened the envelope and took out a sheet of paper. I could see that there wasn't much on it, just a few lines in Caroline's neat handwriting. Em and I stood waiting, watching Dad's face, trying to guess what it was about.

"Well." Dad put the sheet of paper back in the envelope. "That's it. Caroline and I are no longer together."

"*Dad!*" Em's face puckered.

"Sweetheart, don't cry. It's not your fault!" Dad put one arm round Em, the other round me. He pulled us close. "It's nobody's fault. These things happen."

"But you loved her!" Em choked. "You loved her so much!"

"I did," said Dad. "A bit blindly, perhaps. Like some teenager with a crush. I should have seen that we weren't really right for each other. Caroline's a businesswoman. She's sharp, she's practical and I'm just a silly, bumbling professor. I don't blame her for losing patience with me."

"I do!" I declared it very fiercely.

Dad smiled. "You only say that because I'm your dad. Caroline tried her best. So did you and Em! Things just didn't work out."

"It's not because I wouldn't eat meat?" whispered Em.

"Absolutely not! That is entirely your choice. Nobody else's."

"Is Caroline still here?" I said. I stared round the kitchen, as if she might appear at any moment.

"It's all right, you're safe," said Dad. "Caroline's gone. She's moving in with a friend. She'll come by and pick up her stuff in a day or so."

"Oh, Dad, I'm sorry! I'm so sorry!" Em flung both

arms round Dad's neck. "I so wanted you to be happy!"

"I know you did," said Dad. "You both did. But how could I be happy unless we all were?"

"We could have tried more," said Em.

"No." Dad shook his head. "I think you've both tried hard enough. There comes a point where one just has to accept that it's over. You've reached the end of the road."

Eagerly I said, "Does that mean Cass will be coming back?"

Em gave me such a look! Like, *How dare you sound so cheerful when poor Dad is suffering?*

"Sweetheart, I'm sorry to disappoint you," said Dad, "but we can't possibly ask Cass to throw everything up for a second time just to come and mother us. It wouldn't be fair. Not now she's got her life all settled. From this point on," said Dad, "it's up to us. We're going to have to manage on our own. The three of us, together.

Do you think we can do that?" Dad looked at us solemnly. "Do you think we're capable of being real grown-up people who can take care of themselves?"

"Absolutely!" said Em.

Dad said, "Bitsy? How about you?"

Em prodded at me. I said, "Yes! Absolutely!"

I hadn't actually meant that Cass should come back just to look after us. We could look after ourselves! It was just that I really did miss her. But I knew that Dad was anxious.

"No problem," I said. "I can do the cooking, Em can do the housework!"

"Don't quite see why I have to do the housework," said Em.

"Cos you're better at it than I am and, anyway, you can't cook!"

"What about me?" said Dad. "What shall I do?"

I said, "You can put the bins out every week."

"Is that all?"

"Well, and you could make the beds," I said. "You must know how to make beds!"

Dad was starting to look more cheerful. "I think I could manage that," he said. "And I'm a dab hand at washing-up! I might even be able to manage a bit of ironing."

"We'll write it all down," I said. "Who does what. So the place will look lovely when you bring your next girlfriend home."

"Oh, Bitsy, I don't know whether I shall ever have another girlfriend," said Dad.

"You will!" Em said it very fiercely. "We'll make sure you do!"

"Yes, cos you deserve it," I said.

"Well, we shall see," said Dad. "If it happens, it happens."

But only, as I pointed out to Em when we talked about it later on, if we did something to *make* it happen.

"It's no use just sitting back and doing nothing."

"So what do you suggest?" said Em.

"Well…"

"What?" Em sat scrunched up on my bed, with Bella in her arms. "Tell me!"

"*I think we should invite Polly to dinner*," I said. "Like Dad invited Caroline? We'll invite Polly!"

"Mm…"

I could see Em turning it over in her mind.

She nodded slowly. "We could, I suppose."

"Why not? She's our friend! And Dad likes her."

"Caroline said she was mousy."

"That's only Caroline's stupid opinion! *Dad* said she has a good brain."

"He did, didn't he?" Em brightened. "And they do get on well."

"And Polly doesn't have anyone."

"No, she doesn't."

"And Dad doesn't, either. It's a perfect match! All we have to do is get them together."

"You mean outside college?"

"Exactly!"

Em rocked to and fro as she thought about it. Weighing it up. Trying to decide. "Do you really think it could work?"

"No harm in giving it a go. Never get anywhere," I said, "if you don't give things a go."

"That's true."

"So shall we do it?"

"Yes!" Em thrust her hair behind her ears. "Let's do it! I'll call Polly and fix a date."

"A date for Dad!"

"When shall we arrange it for?"

"Friday? That'll give us time to tidy up."

"Don't need to tidy up," said Em. "Polly doesn't care about things like that. Her place is like ours used to be before Caroline came."

"You mean cosy."

"Comfortable."

We beamed at each other. I had a feeling that this was going to go well.

"So what shall we give her to eat?"

"Something veggie."

"Mock steak and kidney!"

"Do we know how to do it?"

"*I* do," I said. "I'm the cook! You can be my assistant."

Meekly Em said, "OK."

"And for pudding—"

"Something nice!"

"For pudding," I said, "I shall make possets."

Nobody, but nobody, could resist my possets. Well, nobody except Caroline. I should have known then that she wasn't going to be right for Dad. Polly was the one!

We'd always loved Polly. I reckoned Dad had too – he just didn't realise it.

"It's up to us," I said.

There was a pause. I thought for a minute that Em was going to get cold feet, but quite suddenly she seemed to make up her mind. She sprang off the bed, tipping a surprised Bella out of her arms. "I'll go and ring Polly right away!"

"Friday," I called, as Em disappeared through the door. "And don't forget to tell her there'll be possets!"

More fantastic reads from Jean Ure...

LEMONADE SKY

When Ruby's mum disappears, Ruby takes charge – Mum's left her and her two sisters alone before. But will they be OK? And can they keep Mum's disappearance a secret until she gets back?

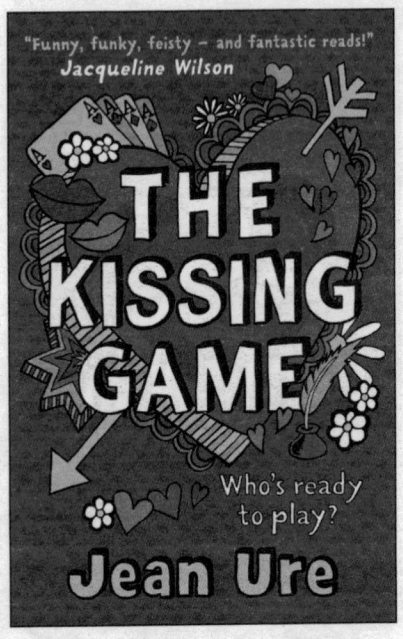

Salvatore d'Amato is determined to get a kiss by his thirteenth birthday. And not just any kiss. A kiss from his heart's desire – the 'lovely, loveable, luscious Lucy'! With his wonderful love poetry, and his secret body-building, how will she be able to resist? If only that horrible Harmony Hynde would stop bothering him in the meantime!

Without Mum, everything is just so *hard*. Things
would be easier if I could just stop feeling; if I could
just freeze, like an ice lolly...

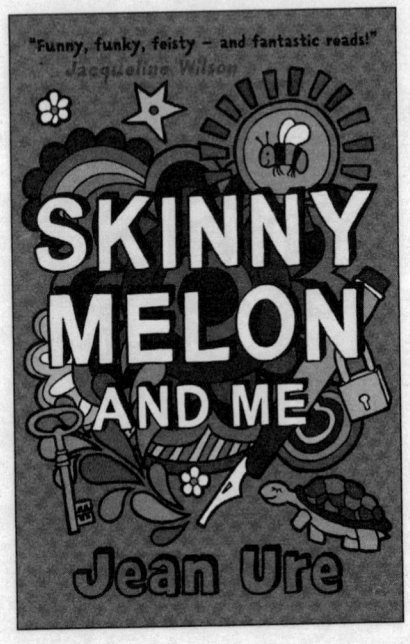

This is the diary of Cherry Louise Waterton.
Problem One: My mum's just remarried a total
dweeb named Roland Butter. Problem Two: I think
she also has a secret too...